9781424208951

Unclaimed treasures

D0053845

Critical Acclaim for PATRICIA MacLACHLAN's Novels

ARTHUR, FOR THE VERY FIRST TIME

"MacLachlan has created a wonderfully original and lovable group of people. The story has a deep tenderness, a gentle humor, and a beautifully honed writing style." —*The Bulletin of the Center for Children's Books*

An ALA Notable Book

CASSIE BINEGAR

"The writing is luminous; romantic ten- and twelve-year-old girls will love it all." —*School Library Journal*

THE FACTS AND FICTIONS OF MINNA PRATT

"A wonderfully wise and funny story that will be read and reread and relished for a long time." —*The Horn Book*

An ALA Notable Book

SARAH, PLAIN AND TALL

"A near-perfect miniature novel." —ALA *Booklist*

Newbery Medal Winner
An ALA Notable Book
Christopher Medal Winner
Scott O'Dell Award for Historical Fiction

SEVEN KISSES IN A ROW

"[A] brief understated story full of humor and the warmth of family caring and mutual affection." —*The Horn Book*

UNCLAIMED TREASURES

"A tender and subtle book that has strong characters, a flowing style, and a perceptive depiction of familial problems and loyalties."

—*The Bulletin of the Center for Children's Books*

A Boston Globe–Horn Book Award Honor Book
An ALA Notable Book

Also by
PATRICIA MacLACHLAN

Through Grandpa's Eyes

Arthur, For the Very First Time

Mama One, Mama Two

Cassie Binegar

Seven Kisses in a Row

The Facts and Fictions of Minna Pratt

Sarah, Plain and Tall

Skylark

Caleb's Story

Three Names

All the Places to Love

Unclaimed Treasures

PATRICIA
MACLACHLAN

A Charlotte Zolotow Book

HARPERTROPHY®
AN IMPRINT OF HARPERCOLLINS*PUBLISHERS*

Unclaimed Treasures
Copyright © 1984 by Patricia MacLachlan
All rights reserved. No part of this book may be used or
reproduced in any manner whatsoever without written permission
except in the case of brief quotations embodied in critical articles and
reviews. Printed in the United States of America.
For information address HarperCollins Children's Books,
a division of HarperCollins Publishers,
1350 Avenue of the Americas, New York, NY 10019.

Library of Congress Cataloging-in-Publication Data
MacLachlan, Patricia.
    Unclaimed treasures.
        p.   cm.
    "A Charlotte Zolotow book."
    Summary: Willa, who wants to feel extraordinary, thinks that she's in
love with the father of the boy next door until she realizes that her "ordi-
nary" true love is the boy himself.
    ISBN 0-06-440189-8 (pbk.)
    [1. Individuality—Fiction.]   I. Title.
PZ7.M2225Un   1984   83-47714
[Fic]   CIP
                                                                    AC

Typography by Joyce Hopkins

First Harper Trophy edition, 1987

Visit us on the World Wide Web!
www.harperchildrens.com

For three Unclaimed Treasures, with love.
Craig, Nancy, and Varnetta Arlene

"I found it!" The tall man stood in the doorway, grinning, holding up the painting for her to see. "In the attic."

"Ah." The woman turned from the window, slowly, carefully. She was very large. Soon she would have a baby. "The apple tree." Her voice was like a sigh. "Just look at the color of the blooms."

The man and woman smiled at each other over the painting.

"And it's still there, that old tree," said the man. He moved to the window to look out over the wide sweep of lawn. He walked with a limp. "Still dying, is it?"

"It was always dying," she said. "You remember. We were always told not to climb it. Warned and shouted at and chased when we did."

The man nodded. "But we had to climb it," he said. "They should have known we had to climb it. Just because it was forbidden."

"It was like a short story, that summer," said the woman, settling in the wing chair by the window. "A short story with a beginning, a middle, and an end."

The man smiled and sat on the arm of her chair.

"Once upon a summer," he began, "there was a tree full of blooms that would soon become fruit, and a pair of twins, a boy and a girl. And the girl wished to do something important and extraordinary."

1

The Beginning

It was a summer that began and nearly ended with a death. One of the next-door aunts died the first week that Willa and Nicholas moved to their new house. The air was still and balmy, and they hung out the upstairs window watching the relatives and friends parade in and out of the gray Victorian house next door.

"It looks like a parade of ants," said Nicholas, hanging way too far out the window. "Aunts, ants. Get it?"

"Yes," said Willa, hanging on to his pants and watching for her true love.

Willa was always watching for her true love, in every line outside the movie theater or ice rink or at the bank. Stopped at a light, Willa always looked over to the next car for him. He would, she knew, be tall and solemn. Solemn. Not like her mother, who was loud and cheerful and wore bright colors. Not like her father, who murmured a lot and rustled his class papers. Willa loved her mother, though she did not understand her. Willa loved her father, too. He was the one who came up at night and nuzzled in Willa's neck and sang songs she knew he made up. They droned some like a hive of bees and put her to sleep. Willa had read in a book once that she might fall in love with her father. So she tried—but she couldn't. She threw herself into his arms once, pressing up close against him, whispering in his ear the way it was done in the movies. He had looked at her strangely, smiling, as if he had read the same book or seen the same movies.

"Great Hoover Dam," said Nicholas in the window. "Will you look at all the long black cars."

Willa smiled. Nicholas was experimenting with bad language, slightly disguised. She squeezed next to Nicky and leaned farther out. Maybe her true love would be an undertaker. The undertakers were dressed in black, and they wore gloves and looked solemn. All except the one who was earnestly picking his nose. None was her true love.

As Willa and Nicholas watched, a door to the side porch next door opened, and a boy came out to sit on the step. He began eating an apple, neatly spitting out the peel as he ate. He looked up and saw them in the window.

"Hi," he called. His hair was fair and hadn't been brushed.

4

"You're spitting out the healthiest part of the apple," Willa called.

The boy nodded, smiling slightly.

"I'm sorry someone died there," said Nicholas kindly.

Willa was horrified. Things like death and pimples and mayonnaise in the corner of someone's mouth were best left unmentioned, she thought.

The boy was not horrified, however.

"It's an aunt," he called up. "A great-aunt. One of the Unclaimed Treasures."

"Unclaimed Treasures?" asked Willa.

"One of the aunts," he said. "Unmarried. Unclaimed. There are two left over," he added. He spit a large piece of apple peel into the bushes. "Why don't you come visit?"

Nicky and Willa looked at each other. Go over next door? Where there was a funeral? For someone they didn't know?

"I've never been to a funeral," whispered Nicky. It was clear he wished to go.

Willa stood up, her face pale.

"But there's a dead aunt over there," she whispered.

Nicholas took her hand.

"Death," he announced, "is not catching, Willa."

And that was the beginning.

The boy's name, it turned out, was an unfortunate one—Horace Morris—though it did not trouble him. He announced it matter-of-factly, calmly, like a weatherman announcing rain.

"I'm Willa Pinkerton," said Willa. "And this is my

5

younger brother, Nicholas." Seven minutes younger Nicky was, since they were twins. But Willa always introduced him as her younger brother. And Nicky, being Nicky, never cared.

"Come on." Horace Morris beckoned them. "There's good food inside." It was obvious Horace Morris liked food. His pants bulged at the pockets, and he had a slight roll over his belt.

Inside, the kitchen had large black and white floor tiles, splendid for hopscotch, Willa thought, and high ceilings and lots of food and people. Everyone there was smiling and talking, including Horace's two aunts— the leftover Unclaimed Treasures. They did not look like any aunts Willa and Nicholas had ever seen before. Though they were great-aunts, ancient and wrinkled, they were dressed in bright colors, and they were drinking and smoking. Aunt Lulu was teetering on lavender high-heeled shoes with many straps that crisscrossed and crept up her legs, ending somewhere under her dress.

"How nice for Horace to have you here!" she exclaimed. "You may try the wine."

The plump one was Aunt Crystal.

"Welcome to the neighborhood," she said. "The former owners of your house did not treat our cats with respect."

Willa noticed that there were two cats on the counter attacking a roasted turkey.

"We have three cats," Aunt Crystal confided. "The two on the counter are named Black and Blue because

6

they fight. Gloria is in the parlor keeping company with Mab."

"Is Mab another cat?" asked Nicky politely.

"Oh no, dear," said Aunt Crystal, smiling and patting his hand. "Mab is the deceased."

Horace handed Willa and Nicholas glasses of wine, and Willa's stomach began to feel uneasy as they moved through the mass of people in the dining room and into the parlor.

"Holy Crisp," murmured Nicky, for he had just spied the open coffin sitting in the bay window.

"Come on in," invited Horace. "If you want you may have a look."

Willa gulped at her wine, and they moved closer. Gloria, a long-haired Persian, was indeed keeping company with Aunt Mab. She was perched just above Aunt Mab's folded hands, preening herself. Aunt Mab was laid out in what was really the music room, right next to the Knabe. She had a mildly sour look on her face, as if she had expected someone to play Schubert or Chopin, but had been presented with Czerny exercises instead.

Willa drained her wineglass nervously and sat on a velvet chair. She had never in her life drunk wine. But she remembered her mother once, after a party, dressed in an India print dress and in bare feet, standing in the kitchen singing three verses of "Bringing in the Sheaves." Her mother had sung it "Bringing in the Sheets," and her father had made coffee and been amused. Willa beckoned to Nicky.

7

"Do I look or sound funny?" she whispered.

Nicky shook his head, then stared again at the coffin.

"Very well, then," Willa said brightly. "I'll have another."

Horace Morris brought her another wine and sat down on a stool.

"Where are your mother and father?" Willa asked him.

"My father is over there," he pointed. "See? The tall one next to Aunt Crystal."

Willa looked, but all she could see were people milling about.

"My mother is not here for a while," Horace went on. "She's gone to seek her fortune." Horace was eating another apple, carefully spitting the peels into a potted plant.

"Seek her fortune?" asked Nicky. Willa knew he had visions of a pig or a dog with a long stick and a kerchief over its shoulder. Nicky was a great reader.

Horace nodded and spit. "She said the Treasures take care of the house and of me. She's out in the world looking for something that needs her."

"That's wonderful," said Willa, staring at Horace. "I wish my mother would do that."

"Our mother is having a new baby," explained Nicky.

Horace was impressed. "She is?" He looked at Willa. "I wish *my* mother would do *that*," he said fervently.

Willa had a sudden and sharp memory of a day last week, just before dinner, talking about the new baby.

"Will it be twins, like us?" Nicky had asked.

Their mother, huge and brightly colored like an air

8

balloon, turned sideways at the kitchen counter to cut tomatoes. She shook her head.

"One heartbeat, the doctor says."

"That's what he said before we were born!" protested Willa, dismayed at the thought of two babies. One was bad enough, smelling and crying and dirtying up the house.

"That was eleven years ago," said their mother. "They know more now."

Willa sipped her wine, thoughtfully. They didn't know enough, she thought, to keep her mother from being pregnant. Her mother should be out in the world doing something important and extraordinary. Like Horace Morris's mother. That's what I will do someday, Willa thought. I know it. Something important and extraordinary. Not like having babies. You just popped babies out and had them on your hands for years.

"Something important and extraordinary," Willa said out loud. "That's what I am going to do. Someday."

"Do the two go together?"

Willa and Nicholas looked up.

"Papa," said Horace. "This is Willa and Nicky. From next door."

The tall man smiled and pulled up a chair to sit.

"I heard about you. From the Treasures," he said.

Willa stared at him. He had a sweet, sad smile, something like Horace's.

"We're sorry about"—Nicky bent his head in the direction of the coffin—"her being . . ."

"Dead," said Horace's father kindly. "Thank you." He looked at Willa again, studying her. "Well, do they?

9

Go together? Things important and things extraordinary?"

Willa swallowed.

"Do you mean," said Horace's father, "going-skydiving important and extraordinary or saving-a-life important and extraordinary or creating-something-beautiful important and extraordinary?" He smiled. "Or just plain everyday important and extraordinary?"

Willa blinked. There was a silence.

"She's drunk, I think," announced Nicky, who had never seen his sister so silent.

Horace's father laughed.

"Have a sandwich, Willa." He turned to Horace. "We'll have to leave for the church soon." He reached out to touch Horace's wild hair, and Willa saw that he had a smudge of blue paint on his wrist. He stood up, looking tall and solemn.

"Come back often," he said to Willa and Nicholas. He went over to the coffin, slowly and gracefully plucking up the cat from inside.

"We'd better go," Nicky whispered to Willa. She nodded.

"Tomorrow," Nicky said to Horace. "We'll see you tomorrow."

He pushed Willa in front of him, through the dining room and into the kitchen. Aunt Crystal was sitting up on the counter, her legs dangling, either Black or Blue batting at the beads around her neck. She waved. Aunt Lulu, cigarette ashes sifting down the front of her dress, opened the door.

"Thank you for coming," she trilled after them. "I'm sure you were a comfort."

Outside it was quiet, still again, as if they had passed from one world back into another. Everything had blurred edges, the apple tree, their mother's phlox, even Nicky walking beside her. Willa knew it was the wine. They looked at each other, and Nicky began to laugh.

"What?" asked Willa.

He pointed to her hand. She still carried her wineglass.

They walked into the kitchen, where their father was making spaghetti sauce, stirring and sniffing and making embarrassing sounds of delight. Their mother was sitting at the table, chopping celery.

"Where have you two been?" she asked them. "Supper's almost ready."

"We have been attending a funeral next door," said Nicky very formally. This caused Willa and Nicky to burst into laughter, and they sat down at the kitchen table, Nicholas snorting into his hand, and Willa whooping. Their mother and father smiled at them and at the wineglass.

Finally Nicholas caught his breath.

"They have Horace Morris over there," he said, wide-eyed. "And Unclaimed Treasures and cats."

And my true love, thought Willa, taking the knife from her mother to help chop celery for salad. Tall and solemn, just as I knew he'd be.

11

2

A gray morning mist hung over the garden and yard, and Willa busied herself with kissing her bedpost. She had drawn lips there long ago, when she was nearly seven and when she and Nicholas had first learned about love and sex and flutterings. It had been right after their LST, as Nicky called it. LST for Little Sex Talk. Nicky had been fascinated and had asked their parents for the most specific details, while Willa had been disinterested in all but the kissing. Kissing, along with what Willa called "long and meaningful looks" and Nicky resolutely called "eyeballing."

"But how did you first know Daddy liked you?" Willa asked her mother.

Her mother smiled. "I could feel him staring at me. I knew he was interested."

"You mean a long and meaningful look?" asked Willa enviously.

"Eyeballing," said Nicky. "He was eyeballing her."

"Nicholas," said their father, smiling slightly, "there must be a better way to express it."

"A long and meaningful look," said Willa, nodding her head.

"Eyeballing," said Nicky softly.

Their father stood up and went to the kitchen to make a drink, a certain signal that the talk was over.

"It was something in-between," said Willa's mother after a moment, her voice startling them with its softness. She stared at a spot over Willa and Nicholas's head. "Something very lovely and in-between."

Her mother's strange look made Willa restless. Uncomfortable. And the realization that her own mother and father had some acquaintance with love and sex and flutterings made her nearly mute. Until then, Willa had thought it all reserved for young people in red cars with racing stripes, or those with picnic baskets.

Even now the thought was troubling, and when thoughts troubled Willa she wrote them on small slips of paper and hid them in her bureau drawers for later. Somewhere, underneath her clothes, along with a pack of bubble gum, there was a small slip of paper that read: *June 7, I know how it is done.*

And now that Willa was nearly twelve, on the edge of the world of racing stripes and picnic baskets and her true love, she had taken to practicing bedpost kissing with more verve. Sometimes Nicholas watched.

"Does it feel queer and exciting yet?" he asked. On his lap lay a recent magazine open to an article that described for those who cared to know it the feelings accompanying kissing.

"Osculation," mused Nicky. "Another name for kissing." He looked up. "Well, is it? Queer and exciting?"

Willa unclamped her lips for a breath. "No," she admitted. "But this is only early practice."

"I think," observed Nicky, "that kissing a mahogany post may be a hindrance."

Willa pushed her lips against the post again, and closed her eyes. She unclamped and looked at Nicky.

"You're right," she said. "I need another human pair of lips." She stared at Nicky.

"Oh no! Not mine!" protested Nicky.

"All right," said Willa. "Not yours."

Nicky peered closely at Willa.

"And not his either," he added pointedly. "He's married."

"Whose? What?" Willa jumped self-consciously.

Nicky picked up his sketch pad and sat cross-legged on Willa's floor.

"You know that I know who you're thinking about," said Nicky. He sketched in long strokes.

"Who?" shrieked Willa, furious. "Who?"

Nicky stopped sketching and turned to look out the window, past the old apple tree, at the house next door.

Willa shrugged. "I just thought he was nice."

"No sir, you didn't just think he was nice," he mimicked her. "You were tongue-tied."

14

"It was the wine," said Willa fiercely. "And the funeral. My first, after all." She began to erase the lips on her bedpost and draw new, larger ones.

Nicky sighed. "All right. A bet, then." He held his drawing out and looked at it. He rubbed a part of the drawing with a finger. "I will bet all my chores for the week that you think he is your true love. I know just how you look when you think you have found your true love."

Willa tried to think of someone else—another possible true love. But they'd only moved to the house a week and a few days ago. The only boy she'd met was Porky Atwater across the street. Porky and his family, who all looked alike. Was it six or seven Porkys she'd met? But Nicholas would never believe that. Porky was only nine and spent most of his time sitting on the curb, sucking Popsicles that made colored trails down his bare chest and into his pants. No, Nicholas would never believe Porky.

Willa brightened. "Horace," she said cheerfully. "It's Horace."

"Horace," scoffed Nicky. "It's not Horace, though you could do much worse. I like Horace. He's honest, and I like the way he eats apples."

Willa frowned. She knew a bet was a bet. There was nothing she would have liked more than for Nicky to lose the bet and have to do her chores—vacuum the living room and her father's study, and make salads all week. Willa hated vacuuming. All the dust and dirt crept back so that you had to vacuum again. But mostly she hated making salads. All that work cutting up, when

15

it was eaten and mixed together under the teeth anyway. Willa always wished that she could put a head of lettuce, a tomato, a cucumber, two carrots, and a stalk of celery on the table and tell people to eat up. Willa sighed. Their bets, though, Nicky and hers, were always honest. Had always been honest and would always be so.

Willa shrugged her shoulders. "You're right. I'll take out the garbage and water the plants and set the table all week." Willa made a face. Setting the table was another tiresome task. The dishes and the silverware just got dirty again in a second. There must be a better way, like eating over the stove from the pots.

"Well," said Nicky, suddenly shy and uneasy. "Well," he repeated, bewildered because Willa had given up so easily.

Willa stood up and walked out of the bedroom and down the hallway to set the breakfast table. Nicky scrambled up and hurried after her. She turned her head to one side, listening. Willa could tell he had more to say just by the way he walked.

"All right, all right," said Willa, stopping so abruptly that Nicky ran into her. It didn't hurt. She wasn't bigger than Nicky, just seven minutes older. And fiercer.

Nicky smiled at her, then held out his drawing for her to see. Willa, trying to appear disinterested, glanced at it casually. Nicholas had drawn Willa, wrapped around her bedpost, her lips puckered. The bedpost, though, had sprouted an array of arms, all pushing Willa away. Willa couldn't help smiling.

16

"That's wonderful, Nicky."

"Willa," said Nicky softly. "There will be trouble, Willa. And you'll be sad."

"Sad, bad," said Willa, turning around again. She walked downstairs briskly, pretending to ignore him. But she couldn't ignore his message. For as sure as Willa knew she was the fiercer twin, she knew now and had always known that Nicky was wiser.

Willa lay on the Oriental rug in her father's study, watching the dust motes move in the sun above her head. The vacuum cleaner lay next to her, a body with a tangle of cord and hose. Willa loved her father's study, the light slanting through the hanging plants, making the calm reds of the rug gleam, touching the piles of papers on his desk. Whenever Nicholas or Willa vacuumed the study they were cautioned not to touch a paper, never to move a book. This warning came after Nicholas had once put the hose in the wrong end of the cleaner and papers had blown in a cyclone of sound. He had stood there, fascinated, a slight smile on his face, until Willa had pulled the plug and their father had plunged into the room uttering words that Willa had not known how to spell to look up in the dictionary. Their father taught writing at the college, and he had cursed his students who had not numbered their pages. He cursed them most days anyway, and later, when he had calmed down, he had told Nicholas that pages out of order improved some of their stories. "Most of them," he had said with a sigh. After that Willa spent hours in his room, reading. She marveled that there could be so many different stories—so many words, names, places.

"You know what?" Willa had said to her father. "If you put all the letters of the alphabet in a box, there is every story ever written. Every story possible."

Her father, surprised, had looked up from his desk. Thoughtfully he had lighted his pipe, making the familiar sucking noises. "It sounds simple enough, doesn't it, Willa?" He had peered closely at her. "You know, I think I will keep letters in a box right here to remind myself how simple it sounds." He leaned back in his chair, puffing on his pipe. "And just how hard it really is," he added.

The box of letters lay on his desk, close to the window of plants. The wooden-backed letters, letters from a printer's tray, lay tumbled inside. Willa opened the lid with one finger and stared at the Z and the B and the F. An A lay on its side; the others were turned over. "Sounds simple . . . but how very hard it is." Willa thought of her father's words. Lots of things were hard and sounded simple. Vacuuming, thought Willa. And making salads. Finding your true love.

A pile of student stories lay on the desk blotter, waiting for her father. Willa picked up the top page and began reading.

It was nighttime. Ted and Wanda stood on the terrace, looking at the stars. Wanda's eyes were on the sky, but Ted's eyeballs rolled all over Wanda's body . . .

Willa smiled and sat down in her father's chair. Sex and flutterings, she thought. And eyeballs. Nicky would like this.

Willa glanced at the vacuum cleaner. She put her feet up on the desk, leaned back, and read. The vacuum cleaner lay silent and forgotten in the sun.

3

"Pssh, pssh." The sounds were clear through the open windows of Willa's bedroom. Half asleep, she thought they were left over from her dream, a dream of Ted and Wanda, bathed in moonlight.

"Pssh, pssh."

Willa rubbed her eyes, raising her head from the pillow, listening. She got up and looked out her window. Across the small, sloping stretch of yard that separated her house from her true love's there was an apple tree, old and gnarled. It had survived years of drought and winter kill and uncertain prunings by the Treasures, though everyone spoke of it as dying. Had spoken of it as dying for a long time, Horace had told Willa.

This morning Horace and Nicholas were frantically chasing the cats. One cat was clinging to the trunk of the apple tree as Horace held her. Willa could hear the scrabbling sounds of claws against bark. Porky Atwater, pushing a wheelbarrow of rags, was coming up the sidewalk, hissing into bushes and trees. Willa grabbed her bathrobe and ran down the back stairs barefooted. The grass was startling and cold with dew, and Willa grinned suddenly with the feel of it. "There's Bella-Marie," spoke an ancient voice, "out for a breather." Willa saw that the rags in Porky's wheelbarrow were not rags. They were Old Pepper, Porky's great-grandfather, a dried apple of a man—nearly one or two hundred years old, Willa thought. He had left his teeth at home, and his mouth fell into his face. He wore a rugby shirt, bright yellow and black, and he looked like an old bee.

"Why is Porky hissing at bushes?" Willa asked Horace, after he and Nicholas had pushed the cats inside the house. She sat beside him on the steps. "And who is Bella-Marie?"

"Bella is Old Pepper's pet parrot," whispered Horace. "And hissing attracts birds. Didn't you know that?"

"Of course I knew that," said Willa grumpily, though she had no idea that hissing attracted anything.

Old Pepper wore all his clothes today. Old Pepper was forgetful and independent and forgiven for all of it. Sometimes he forgot his clothes, though he never wandered naked from his own backyard. He went birding there "starkers," as Horace put it, blending in well with the plants and bushes. "Looking lots like Adam in the first garden, even though he has a mustache and wears half glasses," said Horace. "Innocent, like a naked baby at the beach."

Old Pepper peered up into the apple tree as Porky hissed.

"Aha!" he croaked. "I see you, Bella!"

There was a sudden flapping of bright wings high in the tree. "Bug off!" screeched Bella. "Bella's on holiday!"

"Holiday my foot come home I've got mangoes," exclaimed Old Pepper, who often spoke in run-on sentences. He struggled out of the wheelbarrow, arms flailing. Porky grabbed Old Pepper as he weaved, while Bella shrieked and glared at them from above. The cats were fierce against the kitchen window, tails whipping, eyes wild.

Willa, Horace, and Nicholas ducked under the tree and looked up. Bella peered down at them, turning her head from side to side as she moved nervously sideways on her branch.

"Holiday no mangoes!" she shrieked.

Old Pepper staggered under the tree, nearly stepping on Willa's bare foot. He shook his fist. "Be nice!" he yelled. The effort of shouting and shaking his fist almost tipped him over, but Porky staunchly kept him upright. "Be nice," said Old Pepper, more softly.

"Be nice how do I love thee let me count the ways," answered Bella.

Horace, Nicholas, and Willa burst into laughter, and Bella laughed back at them, flying down to a lower branch. She was a beautiful bird, mostly red with a few touches of green and yellow, almost too bright for the tree.

Nicholas swung easily to the first branch of the tree. "I'll climb up," he called to Old Pepper. "Maybe that will get her down."

"No, no, no, no, no" came a shout from the back door. It was Aunt Crystal, waving her hands in the air. "That tree is not for climbing, Nicholas. It is old and dying."

"Never," added Aunt Lulu, looking over Aunt Crystal's head. "Never. Its limbs are most dead. It is not a trustworthy tree."

"Crazy," muttered Old Pepper, glaring at Aunt Lulu. "My limbs are old and most dead, too. But I am as trustworthy as I ever was."

"Not trustworthy, not trustworthy," repeated Aunt Crystal, shaking her head with her hands over her ears.

"Crazy, never, no," chanted Bella from the tree.

Aunt Lulu held up a warning finger. "Never," she said sternly, "never climb that tree." And then she and Aunt Crystal disappeared into the house again.

There was a silence. Willa smiled at Old Pepper and looked up.

"Beautiful Bella," she called softly. "Come down, beautiful Bella."

Bella stared at Willa for a moment, then, squawking, she flew down and sat in the wheelbarrow, gnawing on the wooden side with her beak.

Old Pepper grinned at Willa, then mumbled his way over to the wheelbarrow and climbed in.

"Dumb bird," he said lovingly, putting his arm

23

around Bella. He waved to Porky. "Let's go, Pork. Take the dumb bird home for a mango."

"Dumb bird," said Bella. "Dumb bird for a mango."

Bella settled into the crook of Old Pepper's arm, and slowly, the wheelbarrow squeaking a bit, Porky pushed them off.

"Holiday," they could hear Bella say.

"We'll take a holiday, Bella," said Old Pepper, nodding his head. "We'll wheelbarrow around the block."

Silently, Nicholas and Willa and Horace watched them. Then Willa sighed, sitting down on the grass, leaning against the trunk of the apple tree.

"What a pair," she said softly. "What a pair."

The back door opened and Aunt Crystal looked out. "All in order?"

"All in order," called Horace Morris. "They've gone."

"Well, then," said Aunt Crystal, letting the three frantic cats outside, "we can get about *our* birding."

Aunt Crystal had changed into boots and ballooning knickers and a billed hat that sat on top of her gray curls.

"Lulu!" she called, her voice high like the last note of a song.

Lulu came around the corner of the house, pulling a wire shopping cart. In the cart were bird books, a blanket, and a huge paper bag. Aunt Lulu, as always, wore high-heeled shoes, though today she wore camouflage pants with them. "I've got the books, the blanket, and"—she waved a thermos at Aunt Crystal—"the punch with a little something fierce."

24

Together they went off, one striding, the other teetering, with an every-so-often hiss at a bush.

Willa grinned and turned to Horace.

"The paper bag?"

"Lunch," said Horace Morris. "A good bird has to
fly over a picnic blanket once in a while, they say."

"What a pair," said Nicholas, repeating Willa's words.

The three of them lay down in the grass, and Willa
turned to look at Nicholas. Nicholas was staring up into
the tree.

"What are you thinking about?" she asked.

"I'm thinking," said Nicky slowly, "that Aunt Crystal
and Aunt Lulu shouldn't have said never."

"Never what?" asked Horace, propping himself on
one side.

Willa sighed, staring up into the leaves again.

"He means never climb the tree," she said. "Nicholas
loves trees. And you never tell Nicholas no."

"You never tell Willa no, either," commented Nicholas, still staring.

Horace laughed and lay down again.

"What a pair," he said.

Willa put her hands behind her head and closed her
eyes. "Be careful, Nicholas," she said so softly that Horace didn't hear.

"Hush, Willa," said Nicholas.

Willa smiled and settled back into the grass. She
thought about Nicholas and his dreams of climbing the
old untrustworthy apple tree; of Aunt Crystal and Aunt
Lulu off birding on their blanket; and of Old Pepper

and Porky and Bella on a brief holiday around the block. She looked over at Horace, and for some strange reason, she was comforted to see that Horace had taken an apple, shined and quite large, from his pocket, and was beginning to eat it, spitting the peels in a neat pile in the grass beneath the apple tree.

4

"Oh Ted," she whispered, her lips brushing the alligator on Ted's sweater.

"Wonderful Wanda," Ted murmured, stroking her sprayed shiny hair and her shoulder, still warm from wind sprints.

"Oh Ted," cried Wanda. "In the moonlight, you look like a Greek god."

"I know," said Ted. "I know."

Willa held the manuscript in one hand, moving the vacuum cleaner idly in the other. Back and forth, back and forth. Willa could not remember ever seeing her father stroke her mother's hair. And in the moonlight, her father always looked happy and comfortable and tired, her mother huge, growing daily like a mammoth firefly.

There was a metallic sound, and Willa knew she had sucked up some paper clips. Paper clips, much like dust and dirt, were the natural by-product of her father's work. Willa turned off the cleaner and went to her father's reference library to look up Greek gods. There was a book dedicated to the subject, large with bold print and pictures. The men, Willa noticed, were muscular with sweet faces and fig leaves. The women had sweet faces, too, and no shirts. They all looked quite content in spite of the shortage of clothing.

Willa sighed at the vacuum cleaner and went over to her father's record player. The record still sitting there collecting dust was her favorite, the Pachelbel Canon. That meant her father hadn't changed the record since she had last vacuumed. Willa turned on the record, and the music, quiet and gentle, filled the room. First position, second position, third, hands reaching, arabesque. Willa danced. The music, as always, made her into something other than Willa. Wanda, perhaps? No, not Wanda, standing in the moonlight, her breath on Ted's alligator. Suddenly, there was Willa's mother in the doorway, huge, smiling. Then she was dancing with Willa. First position, the whale, second position, the elephant, her hands strangely lovely and thin, the hippo doing fifth position, a plié. Turning with Willa. Willa smiling in spite of herself. What a pair, thought Willa, echoing Horace and Nicholas under the tree. Her mother's long hair had come loose from its combs.

There were damp wisps around her face, and her cheeks were flushed. Willa and her mother grinned at each other, and then the final strong chords of the canon came. With a flourish they ended their dance, Willa's mother collapsing heavily in a wing chair by the fireplace, Willa on the floor next to the vacuum cleaner.

"Mama?" Willa caught her breath and sat up. "You're good!"

Willa's mother smiled, and wiped her forehead with the back of her hand. "You know, there was a time when I wanted to be a dancer."

"You?" Willa exclaimed. "You?" she said more softly, struck by the sudden look of hurt on her mother's face.

Her mother nodded, lifting her feet together and studying them over her huge stomach. She turned them from side to side, arching them, pointing the toes. "Yes, me. When I met your dad I was taking four company classes each week."

"Four?" Willa was astonished. "But what happened? Why did you stop?"

Her mother shrugged and tucked her feet under her. "I don't really know that anything happened," she said. "I married your dad. Then I had you and Nicholas." She smiled at Willa. "I didn't know there would be two of you, you know."

Willa stiffened. Is that our fault? she thought. Is that what you really mean?

"But you should have kept on dancing. It's important," said Willa.

"Having you and Nicholas was important, too," said

her mother. "There are different kinds of important, Willa."

Wrong, thought Willa. Wrong. She thought of Horace's mother out in the world doing something important. Something extraordinary. She would be tall and sleek-haired, dancing somewhere, perhaps. Or playing bouncy music on an organ in a restaurant while people ate mushrooms. She would be wearing lavender eye makeup and a fur coat and diamonds the size of apricots. After each performance she would eat chicken salad or toasted cheese sandwiches (Willa's favorites) by candlelight. There would be waiters in red jackets with brass buttons waiting to light her perfumed cigarette in its sequined holder. There would be ice-cream sundaes with sprinkles for dessert (another of Willa's favorites). And a tall, splendid, solemn-eyed man, much like Horace's father but *not* Horace's father, would be there, looking loving over the appetizer.

Her mother's voice interrupted Willa's fantasy. "There are some things you can't do just for yourself, Willa. You have to consider others."

Willa's sudden anger surprised her. "Who?" she burst out. "What others? Us? Nicholas and me? Is it our fault?"

"Oh, Willa, you don't understand," said her mother in her infuriating soft voice. She held out her hand. "You're a bit young, yet." Willa's mother got up heavily, stretching backward, her hands on the small of her back. "We're having dinner guests tonight. It would be nice if you'd help." Yawning, then stopping

30

for a sudden bright smile to Willa, her mother left the room.

Willa was speechless with anger. It filled her body. It was as if her mother had opened a door and then shut it before Willa could look inside. Willa's hands shook as she got up. How can you love someone so much one moment, she thought, then hate them even more the next? Willa stood for a moment. Furious, she turned on the vacuum cleaner with such a vengeance that she spilled a box of paper clips on the floor. For a second Willa hesitated. Then, grimly, she bent down and sucked them up—every one—into the vacuum cleaner, clinking and clanking loudly. Wind chimes blown wild.

By the time Willa began the salad for dinner she had still not lost her anger. She was full of silence as she chopped the celery and sliced radishes. Nicholas, peering sideways at her, knew enough to keep still as he set the table. Finally, Willa could stand it no longer.

"Who's coming for dinner?" she grumped, eyeing the two additional places. "Students?"

Her mother turned at the sink, holding out a bunch of daisies and phlox. "These are for the table, please, Nicholas." She turned to Willa. "Tonight is Horace and Matthew," she announced. "I thought I'd told you."

A moment passed. Matthew. Matthew must be *her* Matthew. She had only known him, until now, as Papa or Horace's father. Or her true love.

31

"Here?" she asked, breathless. The bouquet of flowers blurred, just as everything had the day she met Horace and his father.

Wisely, Nicholas said nothing.

"Yes, here," said her mother, turning the flowers, standing back to study them. "There," she said, smiling. "Just right."

Just right. Just right, echoed in Willa's mind. Slowly, Willa put up her hands to smooth her hair. And then it was too late. The kitchen door opened, and there stood Horace, plump and eager; his father behind him . . . holding flowers. Matthew smiled as he gave the flowers to Willa's mother.

"For you," he said. "From the Unclaimed Treasures and us. And our thanks for the invitation."

"Aunt Crystal and Aunt Lulu are asleep," said Horace, "after a hard day of blanket birding."

"Well, dinner isn't anything special," said Willa's mother. "Only chicken pot pie."

Chicken pot pie! Willa was aghast. She loathed chicken pot pie. Chicken did not belong in a pie. Berries or chocolate did. She looked at Horace, expecting him to look aghast, too. But Horace and his father smiled.

Ted held Wanda's hand all through the soup course, through the salad, through the stuffed artichokes, and into the steak with baked potatoes.

"Steak and moonlight," murmured Ted lovingly.

32

"And you," Wanda murmured back to Ted. "What more could one ask for? What more could one ask for?"

"Chicken pot pie," exclaimed Willa's father, "is my very favorite."

Willa looked at her father, horrified.

"One of mine, too, now that you mention it," said Matthew. He lifted his wineglass and looked at Willa. "What about you, Willa?"

Willa took a breath and looked at Nicholas, who was smiling into his salad plate.

"I truly love chicken pot pie," she said happily. She turned to look at Matthew, lifting her chin. "What more could one ask for?" she said. "What more could one ask for?"

5

Dinner was a blur of images and sounds; glasses raised in the candlelight, silverware clinking against plates, quiet conversation. Willa watched Matthew through the flowers, his face framed by leaves and blooms.

"Winnie's gone for a while," he said.

Willa looked up. *Who was Winnie?*

"Meanwhile, thank goodness for the Treasures, though their experiments with cooking tend to go overboard. Last week it was an overabundance of garlic. This week, what?" He looked at Horace.

"Curry," said Horace, wrinkling his nose.

"Thank goodness for neighbors," said Matthew, raising his glass in a toast to Willa's mother and father.

"Thank goodness for apples," said Horace softly, making them all laugh.

"You're a painter, aren't you, Matthew?" Willa's father leaned over to fill Matthew's glass.

"I am."

"Pictures?" asked Willa, her voice sounding strange to her. She suddenly remembered the smudge of blue on his wrist. His hand on Horace's head.

"Not houses," said Nicholas, next to her.

"I didn't know that!" Willa was indignant. "No one told me."

Matthew put on his glasses and looked over Willa's head. "No one told *me* that there is an artist in *this* house," he said. Abruptly he pushed back his chair and got up. In two long strides he was examining a drawing on the wall. It was a drawing of a figure lying in a field of wild flowers.

"Asters," said Matthew, smiling. "Nice." He looked more closely. "N. Pinkerton." He turned to Nicholas. "Is this yours, Nicholas? Are you N. Pinkerton?"

Willa, embarrassed for Nicholas, expected him to be modest, shy. But Nicholas was grinning broadly.

"Yes. And I've got more if you'd like to see." Before anyone could utter a sound Nicholas was out the door, bounding up the stairs.

Matthew moved to another wall.

"And this one? Is this his, too?"

"That's his, too," said Horace with his mouth full of chicken pot pie. "It's a drawing of the garden before anything grows in the garden."

Matthew folded his arms.

35

"Extraordinary," he said.

Willa smiled. Of all Nicky's drawings, this was her favorite. She loved the long furrows where seeds were planted, the border of wire fencing.

"Like the beginnings of a quilt," Willa had said to Nicholas when he first showed it to her. Nicholas had beamed at her.

"Where's the rest of it?" her mother had asked, and Willa had been furious with her. But Nicholas, calm, had explained that was all there was. Just the way it was. There on the paper.

Willa had exploded. "Why don't you tell her the garden is there, just under the surface, about to come up?"

Nicholas had shaken his head. And his patience with his mother had made Willa even more angry. "She doesn't see it the way I do, Willa," he had explained. "The way *we* do." He had held out the drawing, peering at it. "Mama doesn't see the hidden things, those things under the surface, like seeds or roots or night crawlers." He had looked at Willa then. "Why," he had asked softly, "does that make you so angry?" Willa, her teeth clenched, had felt the sudden tightening in her throat that meant tears. She had stared at Nicholas, unable to ask the question that she wanted to. *Why is it, Nicholas, that it* doesn't *make you angry?*

"Here," said Nicholas, bursting into the dining room, intruding into Willa's thoughts. He pulled his chair next to Horace's father's and handed him a folder of drawings.

Matthew laughed. "Whatever is this, Nicholas?" He

held up a drawing, and Willa saw with a sudden sinking feeling that it was his drawing of her entwined with her bedpost.

"Uh . . . that," began Nicholas, looking at Willa, "is two friends," he finished in a rush.

Matthew looked from the drawing to Willa and back again. He smiled slightly. "Some friends," he said.

Willa's mother got up and peered over Matthew's shoulder. "Why," she began, "that looks a bit like Willa! Willa and her bedpost!"

Willa's face grew hot and she closed her eyes, her hands clenched together in her lap.

"Mrs. Pinkerton." Horace's voice was loud in the dining room. "Could I please have some more of this chicken pot pie?"

Willa opened her eyes. She could feel tears at the corners.

"Why, of course!" Willa's mother was delighted. "Here, Horace. I wish everyone in this house liked my chicken pot pie as much as you do."

The bedpost drawing forgotten, Willa's mother served Horace a helping of chicken pot pie.

Horace looked over his plate at Willa. His eyes were steady and unblinking. And then, one corner of his mouth twitched.

For me, thought Willa with sudden recognition. Horace did that just for me.

"And this is fine, Nicholas," Horace's father went on, delighted. "The color. The reds!" He held it up for Willa to see.

The painting was of Willa, lying on the Oriental rug

37

in her father's study, reading a manuscript. Beside her lay the vacuum cleaner, tangled and quiet like a sleeping snake.

Willa's father smiled and looked over his glasses. "Willa truly loves vacuuming."

"And this." Matthew turned to another drawing. "The apple tree in the side yard."

"The untrustworthy apple tree in the side yard," said Nicholas.

"I know," said Matthew. "I heard what Lulu told you. But she's right, you know. The limbs are old and brittle." He frowned. "Soon the fruit will be on the tree again." He looked up. "Which reminds me that I have a painting to finish. And no model."

"You have a show in the fall, don't you?" Willa's father leaned back in his chair. "I read about it somewhere."

"Papa," said Horace suddenly. "What about Willa?" Everyone turned to look at Horace, who was chewing on a stick of celery.

"What *about* Willa?" asked Nicholas.

"What *about* me?" asked Willa.

Horace's father leaned forward, studying Willa. "Horace," he said slowly, "I do believe you're right. Willa, would you like to sit for me?"

"I am sitting," said Willa.

"I mean for a painting. I need a model. Of course, I would pay you."

Pay me? For sitting?

"That is, if you've nothing more important to do

for the next few weeks. And if your parents don't mind."

"Would you like to, Willa?" her father asked. "It isn't easy, you know."

Not easy? Of course it would be easy. Sitting for him.

"I had started the painting with Winnie—Horace's mother," said Matthew. "But I need a model to finish it."

Winnie. Horace's mother. Gone to seek her fortune.

"It would mean about three morning hours a day. When the light is best."

> *"Ted, Ted, sweet Ted," murmured Wanda. "Come and regard the sunrise."*
>
> *"Wonderful Wanda," exclaimed Ted in wonderful wonderment. "Let me see you when the light is best."*

"Willa." Nicholas poked Willa's arm. "Willa." Startled, Willa looked up to see them all watching her.

"Yes," said Willa. "I guess I can sit for you."

"Well then." Matthew smiled. "We'll begin in a day or two." He turned to look out at the apple tree. "Then I can face the figure in the painting."

"The figure?" asked Nicholas.

"Some painters have trouble with color," said Matthew, his eyes fixed on the tree. "Some with form. Some with content."

"It sounds like my students," said Willa's father

39

wryly, "who have trouble with all of the above."

"My trouble is the figure in the painting," said Matthew. "I cannot seem to get that figure." His voice trailed off. "And the face," he repeated to himself, as if no one else was there.

"When I am an artist," began Nicholas. He stopped because Matthew had turned and was holding up his hand.

"Nicholas." Matthew put his hand on Nicholas's shoulder. "You are an artist. Right now."

"Right now?" Nicholas grinned.

"Right now. And now we must go," said Matthew.

There was talk then, the scraping back of chairs, and they moved from the dining room through the kitchen. Willa walked behind Horace, looking at his father's hand on Horace's shoulder.

Outside the moon was rising, touching the leaves of the apple tree. Matthew and Willa's parents walked across the grass talking quietly of gardens and lawns and the evening. Willa saw her father put his arm across her mother's shoulders.

"Hey, Willa," whispered Nicholas. "Guess what."

"What?"

"I'm an artist, Willa. Right now."

Willa and Horace smiled, their teeth gleaming in the darkness.

"Hey, Nicholas," whispered Willa. "Guess what."

"What?"

"*I'm* a sitter," whispered Willa.

Nicholas sat on the lowest limb of the apple tree, swinging back to look up. Horace and Willa sat on the ground. Horace loosened his belt and lay flat on the grass.

"Hey, Willa, hey, Nicholas," he whispered. "Guess what."

"What?" asked Willa.

"I hate chicken pot pie," whispered Horace Morris. And the three of them snickered and snorted, finally breaking out in shrieks of laughter under the moonlit apple tree.

The woman shifted a bit in the chair by the window. Her back hurt strangely, in a way different from any she had ever known.

She watched the man walk past the fireplace, past the bay window, past the grand piano that sat like a watching dog. He hung the picture of the woman and the apple tree over the fireplace. The woman smiled because she was watching the man's face and he was smiling.

The woman in the painting was young, and wore a white dress trimmed with ivory lace. In her hand was a wide-brimmed white hat with pale-green streamers falling from it like trailing fingers. It was spring, and the tree was laced with white flowers.

"I can almost smell the blooms," said the man.

"That was the summer," said the woman, "that I thought the figure in the painting was me."

"It was; it wasn't," said the man. "It was just like Old Pepper said, 'Things are seldom as they seem. You must do better than just look.'"

"Old Pepper," said the woman, remembering. "It was Old Pepper who told us it was the everyday things that matter. Like morning light, the smell of grass, who you are, what you think, and how you live."

"Simple, everyday things," said the man, and they both laughed.

"Who knew then," said the man, thoughtfully, "that Old Pepper was right?"

43

6
The Middle

"Elephant. It's easy," urged Willa. She sat on the curb-stone with one of Porky Atwater's younger brothers. This one was Jojo, though his real name was Ronald. There were seven brothers and sisters in Porky's fam-ily, and none of their nicknames had a thing to do with their given names. Porky's real name was Eldred, Lala was really Dwight, Goosie was Martha-Corinne, Possum was Chris, and on and on.

Jojo was four years old and couldn't say elephant. It didn't bother Jojo a bit. But it sent Porky into a "decline," as Aunt Crystal called it. Aunt Crystal was an expert in the area of "declines." She told Willa and Nicholas about the mailman who had gone into a "decline" because Aunt Lulu didn't want to marry him. "She loved him for the mail," Aunt Crystal confided to them, "and the mail only. He went into quite a decline after that," she went on. "Legs gave out. Had to be driven on his route."

"Come on, Jojo. Elephant."

Jojo took his finger out of his mouth.

"Elephantent," he announced.

Porky clapped his hand to his forehead and fell over backward on the grass. The beginnings of a decline, Willa thought.

"Too many syllables," said Willa patiently.

"Syllalables?" asked Jojo.

"Syllables," said Willa slowly.

"Don't know 'em," said Jojo. "I want a Popsicle."

"No Popsicles until you say elephant right," said Porky. "Everyone else in the family can say elephant."

"Mean," mumbled Jojo, shoving his entire hand into his mouth.

"It's easy, Jojo," said Willa. She reached over and took Jojo's wet hand out of his mouth. "Say el."

"El," said Jojo.

"Ah."

"Ah."

"Phant."

"Phant," said Jojo, smiling.

"Elephant," whispered Willa.

"Elephantent!" shouted Jojo. "Can I have a Popsicle?"

"No!" shouted Porky.

46

Jojo screwed up his eyes and began to cry, jamming both hands into his mouth.

Willa put her arms around him. "Go get him a Popsicle, Porky. And a handkerchief for his nose goo!" she called after him.

"What's up what's the matter why is he crying?" asked Old Pepper, leaning on his cane. Bella walked behind him, hooked to a chain leash clamped around Old Pepper's wrist.

"He's upset because he can't say elephant he wants a Popsicle," said Willa, realizing she'd just said a run-on sentence.

Old Pepper bent down slowly, slowly, and collapsed in a heap on the curbstone.

"Hush up," he commanded, and to Willa's great surprise Jojo hushed. He took his hands out of his mouth, hiccuping softly.

"Say elephant, Jojo," said Old Pepper.

"Elephant Jojo," said Jojo, sticking his hands back into his mouth again.

"Elephant Jojo," repeated Bella as she hopped down from the curbstone to examine the street.

"He can say it!" exclaimed Willa, amazed.

"Sure he can say it sometimes he doesn't want to," said Old Pepper.

"Just doesn't want to?" asked Willa.

"To," said Bella, tilting her head, her beady eyes on Willa.

Willa smiled and reached out to stroke Bella's smooth back.

47

Willa looked at Old Pepper. "How did you know that?" she asked him. "How could you know that?"

Old Pepper leaned back and put his arm around Bella.

"I did more than just look," he said.

Willa grinned. "You're smart, Pepper."

Old Pepper grinned back at Willa.

"Wouldn't know it, would you?" he said. "By just looking."

Slowly, slowly again, Old Pepper got up. "Come, Bella-Marie. A walk."

Willa watched them move slowly along the street, the metal of the leash between them gleaming in the sun.

"A walk," Willa could hear Bella say as she waddled behind Old Pepper. "A walk."

Porky came running up, two melting Popsicles in his hand.

"Okay, Jojo," he said, sitting on the curb. "Say it like the rest of us."

Jojo unwrapped a Popsicle, stuffing the paper covering in his pocket. The Popsicle was orange, and he licked it in long tongue slurps. He turned to Porky and smiled.

"Elephantent," he said.

"Wonderful Wanda, beautiful Wanda," said Ted.

"Don't call me wonderful," said Wanda, chewing on the long nail of her index finger.

"Look further. Look beneath the surface. Into my soul. What do you see?"

"Wonderful," said Ted. "Beautiful," said Ted.

"You may be right," said Wanda thoughtfully.

The music was clear and sweet and hung lightly in the afternoon air. Aunt Crystal and Aunt Lulu sat on kitchen chairs near the garden, rehearsing. The cats were nearby, one asleep in the sun, stomach skyward, legs up. The others chased butterflies and lurked under the bird feeder, watching for a careless bird.

Aunt Crystal played her viola with gusto and a wandering vibrato, lunging into notes. Aunt Lulu had polished her flute to a gleam, and her foot tapped rhythmically and steadily. She was, it was clear, the metronome of the duet. Bella-Marie, beside herself with delight at the flute, sat under Lulu's chair and rocked back and forth. There was a slight breeze, and the Unclaimed Treasures had clipped the music to the stands with clothespins to keep the pages from fluttering.

"A musical wash," murmured Horace, sitting between Willa and Nicholas. They leaned up against a stone wall where Horace had some apples stored between rocks.

"What are they practicing for?" asked Willa.

"To get better," said Nicholas. He sat, cross-legged, his sketchbook on his lap.

"You know what I mean," said Willa, holding out her hand for an apple.

49

Horace rubbed an apple against his shirt and handed it to Willa.

"They're playing at the opening," he said. "At Dad's show."

Horace pulled his knees up, leaning his chin on them, and looked thoughtful. Willa looked over to her mother's garden and frowned. Her mother, huge and clumsy, was weeding there, moving slowly between the rows on her knees like a giant slug. Willa closed her eyes and leaned back, shutting out her mother. Nicholas's charcoal made soft scratching noises against the paper as he drew. The smell of grass was strong, and a sudden breeze made Willa open her eyes. Willa looked over to the apple tree, and from where she sat she could see the small apples. Just beginning to grow. Two weeks, it was. Two long weeks they had lived here. And in those two weeks Nicholas had become an artist. And Willa had found her true love. And the apples had come. A lifetime.

"You know," said Willa, watching Aunt Crystal and Aunt Lulu, "the Unclaimed Treasures play pretty good."

"Well," corrected Nicholas, as she had known he would. "They play well."

"Well, I know it well," growled Willa. "I always say that wrong. I like good better." She glared at Nicholas.

"Aunt Crystal used to be a famous violist," said Horace. He took a bite from his apple. "She played all over the world."

Willa sat up straight. "Aunt Crystal? She was? Why did she stop?"

Then, just as if she'd heard the word *stop*, Aunt Crystal shrieked and stopped playing, right in the middle of a phrase, the notes left hanging.

"It's a cat," explained Horace. "The cats love to jump after her bow."

"Shame!" shrieked Aunt Crystal. She jumped up and ran after a cat. Blue. She chased him around the back of the garden, shaking her bow over her head. Willa saw her mother straighten up and shade her eyes, watching. Aunt Lulu waited patiently, fingering her flute without sound, as if this were part of the music, a silent cadenza, a bridge to the next theme.

"For shame, for shame!" they could hear Aunt Crystal shouting after Blue, who had disappeared behind the garden, beyond the compost pile, and on past the first line of trees bordering the woods. It was quiet then. And soon, the famous violist plodded back from behind the compost heap, past the garden and into the yard. She stopped, folding her arms on her big chest, glaring at the other cats. Aunt Lulu looked up. And behind her, unseen by Aunt Crystal, Willa could see Blue peeking around the fence post.

Aunt Crystal wiped her forehead, then sat. Aunt Lulu lifted her flute to her lips.

"E," pronounced Aunt Crystal loudly.

And they played again.

Horace Morris sighed, a sound so soft that Willa might not have known except that his shoulders moved a bit. A sad gesture.

Willa reached over to touch him on the arm.

"Horace?" she whispered.

"They miss Mother," he said, looking straight ahead. "They are playing a Beethoven trio." He turned and looked at Willa. "Mother plays the violin. There are only two parts here. They miss her." He turned to watch them play.

Willa's heart moved, a sudden wrenching feeling that was new to her. *They* miss her? Willa took a bite of her apple, watching the sweet, sad look on Horace's face. She turned and looked at her mother, who was standing, her hands behind her, rubbing her tired back. And then, across the yard, the kitchen door opened and Horace's father, a paintbrush held loosely in his hand, came out the door. He stood for a moment, watching the Unclaimed Treasures. Then he sat on the steps, listening. No one else saw him but Willa. No one else saw his look, like Horace's, sad and thoughtful. And the music went on, and Horace reached above his head for another apple, and the Unclaimed Treasures played two parts of a Beethoven trio in the afternoon.

7

The doctor's office was hot, the walls the color of old butterscotch pudding, and it was full of fat women. They shifted and sighed like the ocean as they read their magazines, smiling at each other over the pages. It was, Willa thought, much like an orchestra. Each time the door to the office opened and another woman came in, they all moved and switched places for the new instrument. The doctor's secretary was tall and thin, like a praying mantis, and she had an astonishing hairdo. Willa thought it was bad taste, or at least unkind, for the doctor to hire such a girl to sit in front of all the fat women. They must be all terrifically sad and depressed, though as she studied them they all seemed pleased to be fat. Maybe the world was all turned around, thought Willa. She pressed her fists into her eyelids, and suddenly, unaccountably, she began to feel sorry for the beautiful secretary.

Please, dear God, thought Willa, make the beautiful skinny secretary as fat and swollen as the rest. Make her have varicose veins; make her shift and sigh. Uncurl her hair, God. Amen and over.

It was one of Willa's tests. One of her bargains. *When I turn the corner the next person will be my next best friend. When I look up everyone will be dancing in the streets. If my true love smiles at me I will make salads and vacuum eternally.* Willa opened her eyes and shifted in her seat with the last thought. Willa looked at the secretary, but the poor mantis was as beautiful as ever. She did have a run in her stocking, though she didn't seem to know about it. Perhaps if Willa told her she, too, could be miserable.

Willa's mother moved next to her and turned sideways so that her stomach bumped up against Willa's elbow. Willa stared, half revolted, half curious. Suddenly, her mother's stomach moved to one side, something pushing against Willa's arm.

Willa jumped, still staring.

"Mom! Mom, look!"

Her mother turned a page and yawned.

"What?" she asked, her lips moving silently as she read a recipe.

Willa grabbed her mother's arm.

"Look!" she whispered.

54

Her mother let the magazine fall to the chair, and she stared at Willa.

"Look," whispered Willa, wide-eyed. She pointed to her mother's stomach.

Her mother sighed and closed her eyes for a moment. Willa watched her open her eyes again and smiled slightly.

"The baby's been doing that for quite a while, Willa."

"That much?" asked Willa.

"Sometimes. Soon the baby will become quiet. Not move so much, when it's ready to be born."

"When is that? When *is* the baby coming?" asked Willa.

She looked up at her mother, waiting. And then, a strange look came over her mother's face. A look that Willa had never seen before. The look was far away and it made her mother seem far away, too. It made Willa's throat tighten, and she could feel the hair on her arms stand up. What was it?

Her mother shook her head a bit, then looked down at Willa.

"Three weeks," she said softly. "About three weeks."

"Mrs. Pinkerton?"

Willa and her mother looked up. The praying mantis was beckoning to her mother with a crooked finger. The fingernail was brightly polished. Willa thought of Wanda.

"I'll be back," said her mother.

And then she was gone, leaving Willa with an entire room of sighers and shifters.

Three weeks. In the murmurings of the room Willa was struck suddenly with that. It was too soon. *Three weeks is too soon. I have to sit for the painting. The baby will interfere. I'll have to help. Make dinners. Clean the house. Too soon.* Willa sighed and looked around the room. *Having babies gets in the way of true love.*

The woman in the next chair leaned over.

"Aren't you lucky, dear."

"Me?" asked Willa. No one outside her family had ever called her dear.

"You'll have a younger brother or sister," said the woman, smiling. "You'll share. Sharing is so nice."

Sharing, thought Willa, was not nice. It was low on her list of things to hope for—along with flat feet or bad breath. Maybe she should tell the woman that, so she wouldn't be disappointed when she had eleven children who did not share.

The door opened and Nicholas peered in. And in that moment, for some strange reason, Willa began to feel just as sorry for the woman as she had for the praying mantis. *Please God, make sure all her brats share. Please make sure. Salads, God. Remember I'll make salads.*

"Sharing," she announced to the woman, "is splendid fun." Willa remembered reading that in a horrid children's magazine once. "This is my younger brother, Nicholas. And we share . . . with great joy," she finished in a rush.

The woman smiled and so did Nicholas.

"Two of you sharing," said the woman. "That's nice."

56

"Joyous," corrected Willa. Joyous was a favorite word of Willa's.

"Joyous," said the woman.

They both looked up at Nicholas, and so did everyone else in the room.

"Joyous," said Nicholas, grinning suddenly.

Everyone grinned back at Nicholas, including the praying mantis, who had been typing as if a flood were coming.

When the door to the doctor's inner office opened and their mother came out, there was an entire room of grinning sighers and shifters, one praying mantis, and Willa and Nicholas.

"Good-bye," Willa told the room.

" 'Bye."

"See you, dear."

Outside, Willa's mother raised her eyebrows at them as they grinned down the hall.

"What was all that about?"

Willa and Nicholas laughed. They put their arms out, reaching behind their mother's back.

"We're sharing you, Mom," said Willa, grabbing onto Nicholas's hand. They pulled her with them, half running down the hall to the elevators.

"Well, you two sound happy," she said, and for a moment her voice sounded happy, too.

"Joyous, Mom," said Nicholas.

"Joyous," said Willa, listening to her voice bounce off the marble walls.

Two people waiting for the elevator smiled at them as they waited.

Willa looked up to see her mother smile back. She looked almost, but not quite, joyous.

It was late evening, after the dishes had been cleared and washed and put away, when Willa found the picture that made her mother cry. She was cleaning out her mother's purse, a huge bag that was always a tumble of money and wrappers and clipped articles. Once there was one earring at the bottom, the mate never to be found. When Willa was little she used to wear the earring on a chain around her neck.

"What's this?"

It was not an earring that Willa held up. It was a picture. A strange picture, blurred and vague like a dream.

Nicholas looked up from the table where he was drawing. Their father looked over Willa's shoulder. And Willa's mother began to cry. Silently at first, then sobbing, her shoulders shaking.

Willa and Nicholas stared. Their father went over and put his arm around her, bending close to her, whispering in her ear. But she kept on crying.

Nicholas got up, moving over to where Willa stood, and gently took the picture out of her hand.

"A baby," he said after a moment. "*The* baby. It's a picture of the baby."

Willa stared at the picture.

"How can you tell?"

Nicholas smiled.

"I am good"—he looked at Willa—"at seeing things

beneath the surface. Remember? Like seeds and roots and night crawlers?"

Willa looked. Gradually, she began to make out the figure. A head, an elbow, an arm. Willa thought of the baby pushing against her arm that afternoon. Just that afternoon. Willa held her breath. *This baby*.

Willa's father looked up.

"It is called a sonogram, taken with a machine in the doctor's office. It shows us where the baby is in the mother." He tightened his arm around her mother.

"Mama's a little worried," he said. "About the baby."

Worried? Worried about what? It is only a baby, small and soft. What is there to worry about?

"Things can happen sometimes," their father went on. "Mama is older—it's been almost twelve years since she had you. There's more risk."

Risk?

"Mama's had tests. We know the baby is healthy." He pointed to the picture. "And this lets us know if the baby is in the right position to be born. And if it will be a safe birth."

Safe birth?

It had never occurred to Willa that anything bad could happen. She looked at her mother, who was blowing her nose. And all of a sudden the same cold feeling came again—the one that had made her throat close in the doctor's office.

You must do better than just look. Old Pepper's words came back to her.

In that moment Willa knew exactly what the feeling was her mother felt.

She's afraid. Willa looked down at the picture. *In my mother is this baby. Tiny, curled? Asleep? Awake? Brown-haired like me? Like Nicholas?* And a thought came that Willa had never allowed before.

It is real. The baby is real.

8

The white dress was beautiful. It made Willa feel beautiful. She tried it on while the Unclaimed Treasures whispered and oohed and threw up their hands in excitement. The material was stiff against her bare legs. The high lace neck made her feel tall and stately.

"She looks like—"

"Never mind now." Aunt Crystal's voice was sharp.

"The spitting image of—"

"So," interrupted Aunt Crystal, glaring at Aunt Lulu, who might, thought Willa, be going into a decline, "the hat does not have to fit, dear." Dear again, thought Willa. Two times she was dear in two days. "You hold it in your hand, like so." Aunt Crystal posed, holding the hat by her side, trailing the ribbons, looking like a plump old woman in love.

"Beautiful," murmured Aunt Lulu.

And then Horace's father came, looking distracted. He stopped and stared at Willa for one moment, opening his mouth as if he might say something. But then he shook his head and took her hand, leading her up the stairs to his attic studio, talking all the while. Willa looked at her hand in his. Though his hand felt cool, her own hand was hot.

"You look fine, Willa. Fine. Now I'll put you over here by the window." And he placed her where a slight breeze came in the window, rustling the ribbons of the hat and lifting her hair. She had never been in his studio before, and she was surprised to see that the limbs of the apple tree outside crawled up onto the roof.

The room was filled with canvases and cloths and the smell of paint. Along one wall there were paintings neatly stacked, the painted sides facing the wall. But as Willa slowly scanned the room, she saw that some of the paintings had fallen over. Some leaned against each other, precariously, like a set of dominoes. One painting lay on the floor, ignored. Another on a large easel facing Willa—the only one she could see from where she stood—was gray and beige with a blurred figure in the middle. Willa narrowed her eyes, trying to bring the painting into focus. The breeze pushed her hair across her cheek, and Willa felt a chill. A sudden sadness. She shook her head and pushed her hair back, trying to push the feeling away, too. It was a feeling coming much too often lately. Hard to chase away. "And you'll be sad," Nicholas had warned her when he had first learned that Matthew was her true love. And Willa *was* sad.

She watched Matthew, his brow furrowed, mixing paint and whistling softly to himself. And then, across the room, Willa saw a girl in a long white dress, standing still as stone. Willa held her breath as she stared at herself in the mirror. The dress made her look taller, older, even though she knew that the Unclaimed Treasures had taken up the hem, carefully cutting off the lace edges and sewing them back for her. Slowly, she straightened and lifted her chin. The dress was beautiful. The girl in the mirror was beautiful. *Then what was wrong?*

"Here." Willa looked up as Matthew reached around her back, his breath soft on her cheek as he adjusted her arm. "Lean your arm along the windowsill, Willa. Pretend it is the lowest limb of the apple tree. Covered with blooms."

As Matthew leaned back to smile at Willa she suddenly knew what was wrong. She could still feel where he had touched her arm. Where his breath had brushed her cheek. She looked over to the mirror.

Under this dress is me. One small person. Not tall, not stately. Willa Pinkerton.

"Tilt your head, please. Look at me," said Matthew. "Ah, good."

Good. In her head Willa repeated Matthew's words. Like Bella repeating Old Pepper's words.

63

"Nice, nice, Willa," Matthew called to her from behind the easel.

Nice, Willa.

The minutes went by. The dress scratched against her legs, but Willa didn't move.

"Smile a bit, Willa. Just a little. As if . . . as if you have a secret."

Smile a bit, Willa. I do have a secret.

Willa smiled and smiled and smiled as the light moved higher in the sky. The room was filled with silence, and Willa closed her eyes. *Where are you, Ted? Wanda?* Willa thought of the baby—real and moving inside her mother. Hidden, like Willa under the dress.

"Turn your head, Willa. Look at me."

I love you, thought Willa. She turned and opened her eyes, watching Matthew. *I love you.*

Matthew rubbed his face with the back of his hand. Willa looked at herself in the mirror.

One question, please, Horace's father. Who will the figure in the painting be? The girl in the mirror? Or the girl under the dress?

The eyes of the girl in the mirror stared blankly back at Willa. There was no answer.

The moon came in the window. It touched the covers on Willa's bed, making it into a sea. The mirror over Willa's table glowed. Willa's feet hurt. She got up, sighing, and walked out into the hall. The house was quiet, only a small light burning above the stairs. She stood in the hallway, curling her bare feet on the rug, thinking about the studio and the dress. And sitting. Sitting?

64

Willa hadn't sat at all. She'd stood for hours. Stood in the silence until the backs of her legs were stretched and tight, her shins ached, and her head reeled. Why did they call it sitting? Willa walked down the stairs, her hand gliding along the banister. She passed through the dining room, where the bouquet of flowers stood in the moonlight, past the hum of the kitchen. The door of her father's study was open, a lamp lit inside. Willa pushed the door open with one finger. Her mother was sitting in the wing chair, reading, her feet curled under her. She was smiling slightly, slowly twisting a lock of hair in her finger. She looked happy. No, not happy. Not joyous, certainly. But content.

Her mother looked up.

"Willa? Not sleeping?"

Willa shook her head, touching her mother's outstretched hand. She sat on her father's desk chair.

Her mother sighed. "I can't sleep either." She looked at Willa. "Too fat to sleep."

Willa grinned and her mother grinned back.

"Willa," her mother began, "about the other night. My crying."

Willa pushed her hair behind her ears and sat, listening.

"I didn't mean to worry you. Having a baby is such an important thing. So important that sometimes I try to forget about it—push it away. But it always comes back." Her mother took something from between the pages of the book she was reading. "And this brought it all back."

It was the picture of the baby.

"Most times the baby seems so far away," her mother said. "Not really there, you know. But the picture . . ."

"Made it real," said Willa. Like seeds and roots and night crawlers, she thought. Like Nicholas's picture of the garden.

"Why, Willa," said her mother, staring at her. "I guess you're right." And Willa realized that she had spoken her thought out loud.

"I never thought about you much before you were born, you and Nicholas," said her mother, leaning her head against the back of the chair. "But when you came I was so overjoyed. I can remember crying."

"Overjoyed?" Willa sat up. "You mean joyous?"

"Yes, Willa," said her mother, smiling. "Joyous."

"Even though we kept you from your dancing?"

"Dancing? Willa, what are you talking about?"

"You said you didn't dance anymore after we were born. Remember?"

Willa's mother leaned forward in her chair.

"But Willa, that was my choice. I didn't want to dance then. I had you and Nicholas. I was . . ." Her mother waved her hand, trying to find the words. "I was . . . joyous."

Willa frowned. *So much joy over two small babies? Just Willa? Just Nicholas?*

"Mama?"

"Yes."

"When this baby comes I can take care of it sometimes, can't I?"

"Of course, Willa."

"Then you can dance," said Willa.

66

Willa's mother looked at her for a long time. Her eyes filled up.

Please God, thought Willa, don't let her cry. Please. I'll vacuum the living room. The study. The backyard!

"That is a wonderful idea," said her mother very steadily. "A gift."

Her mother handed her the picture of the baby.

"Now I'll give you a gift. Meet your sister, Willa."

Willa looked at the picture.

"Sister? Maybe it will be a brother."

Her mother shook her head. "No, I know. The doctors and your father and I know. Because of a test. It is a girl. And"—she looked at Willa—"she will be . . . she *is* your sister."

Upstairs the door to Nicholas's room was open, a slice of moonlight cutting across the hallway. Willa stood over him, watching his chest rise and fall. The bedcovers were neat and smooth around him. His lips were slightly parted in a smile. The room was cool, the curtains billowing, and Willa hopped from one foot to the other. She hugged herself and shivered, wishing him awake. She coughed loudly. She leaned against the bed and pushed the mattress three times. Nicholas didn't move.

For a long time Willa stood there, watching. For a long time she thought about kissing him.

She didn't.

"Wake up, Nicholas!" she yelled at the top of her voice, nearly overcome with joy. "We've got us a sister!"

9

I love you, Matthew.

It was early in the studio, and through the open windows Willa could hear the Unclaimed Treasures playing near the garden. The cats were on the roof peering in and making growlings; soft, warm sounds.

"When can I see the painting?" asked Willa.

"Later," murmured Matthew. "Not yet."

"Why don't you just take a photograph?" Willa surprised herself with the question. Her voice sounded loud in the studio quiet.

"What, Willa?" Matthew was frowning, his hands making quick brush strokes on the canvas. "What?"

"A photograph. Why do you need me here?"

"A photograph," mumbled Matthew, concentrating. "A photograph," he said brightly as he stood up. He thought.

"Wanda, Wanda, stand with the sun in your face," said Ted with adoration in his voice, a camera in his hand, and well-pressed pants.

"A photograph," said Matthew, interrupting Willa's thoughts, "is the camera's eye. I need my eye. My eye of you."

Willa frowned.

"Don't wrinkle your forehead," said Matthew.

Willa concentrated on not frowning. It made her stomach hurt.

"What *is* your eye?" asked Willa, thinking fiercely of a smooth forehead.

"I don't know yet," said Matthew, peering at his painting, then at her.

"Don't know!" Willa stared at him. "You mean you don't know what I look like?"

Matthew sighed and straightened.

"I mean," he said in a fierce tone of his own, "that I cannot tell now how the painting will look. It may not look the way you think you look. The way *I* think you look. There are," he added more softly, "many things that get in the way between the time a painting is started and it is finished."

"Like what?"

Matthew picked up a cloth and wiped his hands. "Feelings, moods. Things hidden."

"You mean things under the surface!" announced

69

Willa so loudly that Matthew burst out laughing. "My life is full of things under the surface!" She scratched her leg. The material of the dress was irritating.

"It is the same for all of us." said Matthew, stretching, then wearily rubbing his own tired back.

He is, I suppose, thinking about Winnie gone to seek her fortune, thought Willa.

> "Weary Wanda," murmured Ted, "let me rub your weary Wanda back."
> "Higher, Ted," said Wanda, sipping her iced seltzer.

"Someone should rub your back," said Willa, startling herself with the suggestion. She felt her face flush with embarrassment.

But Matthew was not shocked.

"Someone should, you are so very right, Willa," he said.

"Someone will soon," said Willa, feeling bold and warm and in love.

And as it turned out, Willa was right.

"A girl!" Horace Morris was amazed when Willa and Nicholas told him about the baby. He stretched his legs out over the curbstone. "That's something, isn't it? I mean, knowing." He peered at Willa, who smiled at him.

"We got girls at our house," said Porky, sucking his Popsicle.

"All over the place," agreed Old Pepper. "You could have one if you wanted. No one would notice."

70

"Have you got sisters?" asked Nicholas.

Old Pepper nodded. "Enough. Seven of them. I was nearly lost and drowning in stockings and underwear and curling irons, too, when I was young." He squinted his eyes and peered at the roof across the street. "Parrots are better," he said, watching Bella-Marie strut across the roof of the house. "She lives in her clothes. We'd all be better off if we did the same."

Willa thought about the long white dress, about living in it, being forever tall and stately and beautiful. Fit for a painter's brush. *Fit for the painter.* And suddenly the thought of the painting being completed struck her with such a force that she felt chilled. Just as, every so often, the thought of her own death would make her stop, breathless, until she could will the thought away. No more mornings in the studio. Just Matthew and Willa. In the sun-filled room.

Nicholas leaned over and touched her shoulder.

"Willa? What's wrong?"

Willa looked up at him, sitting beside her on the curbstone. Looking up? It came to her just as suddenly as the thoughts of death and the finished painting. She was looking *up* at him.

"You are," said Willa wearily, "taller than I am. For the first time, ever. When," she whispered sadly, leaning toward Nicholas, "did that happen?"

Nicholas, seeing her face, didn't speak. He let her lean on him. And they all watched Bella-Marie, touched by the sunlight, move back and forth across the roof, dressed in her own eternal clothing.

———

71

It was Old Pepper at last, Old Pepper and Nicholas talking in their wise ways about change and dying— in the most matter-of-fact manner—that made Willa decide to do something extraordinary. It had never seemed so important as when she listened to them talk.

"I will die before Bella-Marie," mused Old Pepper, sitting out near the garden, wheelbarrow close by, Bella bumping around the yard. "Certainly I will."

"No," said Willa loudly. Bella-Marie looked up.

"Ah, Willa," said Old Pepper gently, "it's all right, child. It is, after all, my life. I don't mind."

I don't mind. Such a mild answer, she thought, when faced with the prospect of dying.

"Bella's a parrot, they're long-lived," he said.

And he and Nicholas talked softly, their heads close together, deciding Bella's fate while Willa agonized over Old Pepper's dying, and Bella's and her mother's and father's, and the Unclaimed Treasures' and Horace's and Nicholas's and Matthew's—and at long last the worst death—*hers.*

"I myself," stated Nicholas, his voice clear, "wish to be buried standing up. I hate to lie down."

Willa's eyes widened, and in spite of herself, she burst into laughter. Remembering that when they shared a room it was always Nicholas who went to bed sitting up. It was she who welcomed nighttime, closing her eyes with secret thoughts when the lights went out. It was the thump of Nicholas in the upper bunk, falling over at last from his upright vigil, that signaled it was time. Willa would smile, turn over, the covers close about her neck, to sleep for the night.

"Upright," said Nicholas, "or perhaps leaning against a tree so as not to fall over." He looked at Willa. "Or with oversize shoes, long at the front and back to keep me upright."

"Like Daffy Duck," said Horace Morris softly. "And with dried apples nearby, and books . . ."

"Maybe a painting or two," said Nicholas, "like the Egyptians—pictures of things loved to send you off. . . ."

Willa listened, their words bringing death closer. A death every few minutes, a birth every few minutes— something she had heard once on the radio. The baby was coming—a birth. Would a death follow? It was time. Time to do something extraordinary.

The Unclaimed Treasures were near the garden arguing about tempo. Her mother was in the garden *again*. Would she *root* there? Her father was keeping close watch over Ted and Wanda. The light in the upstairs studio was on. Matthew painted on and on. Old Pepper and Nicholas talked of death and parrots.

What was ordinary? What was not?

10

Thoughts of things extraordinary filled Willa. They washed over her at night, waking her in the moonlight. They touched her as she stood with Matthew in the attic room, watching him watch her. After a while, she would turn her head, ever so slowly, to look at the beautiful creature in the mirror. She was always startled to see the girl in the long white dress, even though she willed herself not to be startled. Watching the two thirds of a trio practice faithfully each day in the garden kept the thoughts alive; and seeing Old Pepper nod to himself under the tree, as if agreeing with his own thoughts of death, nearly overwhelmed her. Her own mother, too, was a constant reminder of things extraordinary. Or were they things ordinary?

Willa began asking.

"Ah, extraordinary, let's see," murmured Aunt Lulu, leaning forward, her flute under her arm. "Playing all the sharps and flats," she finally answered with a sideways glance at Aunt Crystal.

Aunt Crystal disagreed, shaking her head vigorously.

"A glossy ibis," she pronounced.

"A glossy what?" asked Willa, staring.

"Good writing," said her father, leaning back in his chair, pipe smoke circling him. "A good paragraph. A good sentence!" he nearly shouted in growing frustration, making Willa jump. She saw the manuscript of Ted and Wanda on his desk.

"Happy children," said her mother, pausing by the back door, her basket full of carrots. "Happy lives. Why?"

"Peace," said Old Pepper, lounging in his wheelbarrow.

"Peace," agreed Bella-Marie.

At last Willa began a list at a neighborhood picnic. There were long tables with red-checked tablecloths that rippled in the breeze. And baskets of breads and fruit. Willa's parents and Matthew sat in the shade of the apple tree, their voices soft. The Unclaimed Treasures tuned by the garden. Old Pepper sat on a picnic bench, peeling an orange in one long and perfect spiral, Bella pulling the end gently with her beak. All shapes and sizes of Atwaters spread out about them.

Willa's list was a two-columned list.

Things Ordinary   Things Extraordinary

Under *Ordinary* Willa listed eating. At once there was more disagreement.

"Eating is extraordinary," said Horace, his mouth full of apple.

"No," said Nicholas. "Eating is everyday. Like sleeping. Going to the bathroom."

"Going to the bathroom can be extraordinary," said Horace, thoughtfully.

"Eating is ordinary," said Willa firmly. And the list went on.

Things Ordinary
1. Eating
2. Sleeping
3. Bathroom
4. Chores

"Chores can be extraordinarily important," said Willa's father. Willa smiled. Her father loved washing the clothes. She would find him, often, leaning over the washing machine as it agitated. "Do you know," he once announced in great awe, "that some washing machines are up-and-downers, and some are back-and-forthers?"

"Washing clothes is ordinary," said Willa's mother with feeling.

"Extraordinary," said Willa in a loud voice, "is as follows." Her father smiled.

"One, Flying. Two, Becoming king. Three, Finding your true love. Four—"

"Wait a minute," called out Old Pepper, struggling to sit up straight. Willa sighed.

"Flying is not at all extraordinary for Bella-Marie. Right, Bella?"

"Bella," said Bella.

Willa glared at Old Pepper.

"And," he went on, holding up a warning finger, "someone falls in love every single *day*." He emphasized the last word. "Every single *minute*."

"Popsicles" came the faint suggestion of Porky Atwater under the picnic table.

"Elephantents?" called Jojo.

Willa tossed her list on the ground, furious.

"How will I ever know?" she grumped, stomping off to the nearby garden to eat tomatoes. The only thing they'd all agreed on was that the ants at the picnic were extraordinary. Willa sat between two rows of tall tomato plants, thinking. The sun was warm, the dirt dry under her.

"Maybe"—Old Pepper's wrinkled face popped up over the second row—"the answer is that ordinary and extraordinary are the same thing. Morning light? The smell of grass? Who you are and what you think and how you live?"

Bella-Marie stared up at Willa. Willa leaned back and closed her eyes.

"And something," said Old Pepper, "will let you know which is which for you when the time comes."

Willa's eyes flew open.

"What? What something?"

"I wish I could remember," said Old Pepper, yawning. "I am presently tired and plan to go to sleep."

And that is what he did, falling over peacefully between the rows of tomatoes in the warmth of the garden.

It was unbearably hot and still in the attic room, even though it was early.

"Three or four more mornings at the most, Willa," Matthew murmured, standing back to peer at his work. "Nearly done."

Only three more mornings. Willa hadn't even seen the painting yet. How could it be nearly done? She had come to depend, count on these mornings. Her time in the attic room shaped her days. Her life. Like eating. Like sleeping. Like going to the bathroom. Willa studied Matthew. He was, she decided, both sad and excited at the same time. Willa smiled, aware that she, too, felt Matthew's own mixture of sadness and excitement.

"What makes you smile?" he asked, brush poised in his hand.

Willa shook her head slightly.

"I was thinking about ordinary things," she said, turning to look out the window at the garden and the wide slope of yard and the tree full of apples.

"Ted, Ted," murmured Wanda. "You are truly extraordinary. Your face, your hair, your eyes like prunes stewing . . ."

Willa felt herself smiling again.

"What is extraordinary for you?" she asked in the silence. "A finished painting?"

"Yes, that," said Matthew brightly, leaning back to look at her. "But more, too." He sighed. "Too much more to even begin talking about here," he added softly. And the sad look came back, around the eyes and the mouth.

I wish I could remember, Old Pepper had said. But you'll know. I know I know something, Willa told the beautiful girl in the mirror. But I don't know what it is I know. Presently, that is, she added, echoing Old Pepper.

Her thoughts caused Willa to raise her chin a bit. Defiantly. Fiercely. Matthew looked up and stared at her for a long time. Willa never noticed.

Silence filled the room. A fly crawled up the back of Matthew's easel. Though she didn't know it yet, Willa was on the edge of knowing. And soon she would know, mostly because of two strangers not yet met. Two people, unrelated, who would never come to know one another, never even hear the whisper of each other's name. As is the way of life sometimes. As is the way of things ordinary and things extraordinary.

"What is this?" asked the man, bending over an attic box. "Pieces of paper only. A bunch of them." He looked at the woman who was sitting, peering over her huge stomach at her toes pointed in front of her.

"A torn-up list," she answered without looking up. "A very important torn-up list."

"Why is it torn up if it is important," asked the man, "or shouldn't I ask?"

"It is important because it is torn up," said the woman patiently.

The man laughed.

"Shades and memories of Old Pepper." He began to read: "One, Flying. Two, Becoming king—"

"Three, Finding your true love." The woman said the words as he did.

"And what about this?" he asked. He held up a small torn edge of a paper. On it the woman could see four letters printed. ILLA.

The woman smiled.

"That," she said, shifting in her chair, "has to do with something very extraordinary I did once upon a summer when there was a tree full of blooms that would become apples, and a pair of twins, a boy and a girl . . ."

11

The End

It was vacuuming time again in the study with the sun and the plants and the smell of her father's pipe. Willa was bent over the desk, reading:

> *"Ted, Ted," cried Wanda in a distraught manner. "Tell me I am the stars, the moon, the universe to you."*
>
> *"All of the above, Wanda dear," said Ted, trying to keep his pipe lit.*

Willa frowned. There was something here. A hint of something familiar. And it did not have to do with vacuuming, or the painting nearly finished, or the baby due in ten minutes or a week. *What is it I know that I know?* A sudden movement parted the curtains, and Willa saw Bella-Marie perched on the windowsill.

"Bella." Willa leaned over the desk. "What brings you here?"

"Bella," repeated Bella-Marie, grabbing at the curtain with her beak.

Willa grinned, then frowned again, sitting in her father's chair. She leaned on the manuscript. Something was just out of grasp. Something.

Sighing, Willa went to the closet and stood on her head, leaning her legs up against the door. The blood began to fill her head, making her wiser.

"Wait, stay like that," said Nicholas, suddenly sitting cross-legged in front of her. He opened his sketch pad and began drawing.

"Your nostrils are hugely awful upside down," commented Willa.

Nicholas smiled.

"Something like the Carlsbad Caverns," she added, feeling full of words and ideas.

"Wise Willa," said Nicholas, drawing furiously. "Becoming wiser by the minute."

"Yoo-hoo." A small voice came from the doorway. Nicholas looked up.

"Oh, stay, stay," the voice said. "I see you are in the midst of an artistic endeavor."

Something. A touch of something known.

The girl moved into the room, bringing with her the scent of something strong and sweet. A bush of honeysuckle?

84

Nicholas's jaw dropped open.

"One more cavern," said Willa softly, not moving from her upside-down perch.

"I am looking for Dr. Pinkerton. Ted," said the girl. She was astonishingly tall. Her legs, from Willa's view, went up and up and up until they turned into blouse and necklace and huge earrings and a head of red hair.

"Our father," began Nicholas, and Willa snickered at the thought of Nicholas beginning the Lord's Prayer.

"Our father," continued Nicholas, glaring at Willa, "should be home soon."

"Oh," the girl's tiny voice peeped. "Children? Ted has children?"

"We are two of a grand array of many," said Willa, still upside-down.

"Many?" peeped the girl uncertainly. Under her arm was a picnic basket. "I have an appointment for sometime this wonderful afternoon to talk about my writing. I thought that we'd amble down to a gentle stream for our talk. I think there is a gentle such stream somewhere close by."

A picnic basket. A gentle stream. Willa felt herself growing into the wisest thing in the world. *Was everyone in love with everyone else?*

"There is," said Willa in a clear voice, "the sewer outlet down in back."

Nicholas stared.

"The rest of the children should be down there," she added.

"The rest?" asked the girl, frowning.

85

"The other dozen," said Willa, "waiting for word of the grandchild."

The girl stared.

"Grandchild?"

"Yessir," said Willa, feeling like the wisest person in the entire world. Greater than the stars, the moon. The universe.

"A grandchild should be here in ten minutes or a week."

"Ted's?" squeaked the girl.

Nicholas smiled.

"Stay," offered Willa kindly. "I'm sure he'll give you a cigar, too. A symbolic gesture."

"No," said the girl sharply, moving toward the door. "I'll go along now." She paused in the hallway and waved her fingers. And then she was gone, the only sign of her the lurking stench of honeysuckle. There was a silence.

"I never," said Nicholas slowly, "ever thought about Dad's name being Ted when you read me the Ted and Wanda story."

Slowly Willa let down her legs and stood up, reaching out her hand to Nicholas to steady herself.

"Good-bye, Ted, good-bye, Wanda," she said.

"Good-bye, Ted, good-bye, Wanda," echoed Bella-Marie in the window.

One stranger met.

"You told her what?" exclaimed Willa's father, dropping his pipe and sending sparks everywhere. "No, sit still," he ordered Willa's mother, who was laughing

86

so hard she couldn't get up anyway. He stamped around the rug.

"Willa had been standing on her head," explained Nicholas. "She took care of everything."

"I'll bet you never ever noticed her long, meaningful looks," said Willa to her father.

"Eyeballing," said Nicholas.

"I noticed her writing," said Willa's father, trying to keep his pipe lit. "I noticed *that* all right! Witless love," he murmured.

Willa sighed.

"I loved it at first," she said wistfully. "Her writing. It was full of eyeballs and sighs and murmurs. Just like love."

"Except," said Willa's father, "the extraordinary parts of love."

Willa stared at her father.

"There *you* go," she groused. "Ordinary, extraordinary. Which is which?"

"You'll probably know," said her mother. "When the time comes."

"What time?" exclaimed Willa. "Now *you* sound like Old Pepper."

Willa's father grinned broadly.

"Get on outside, the two of you. So I can sit here in peace. Quietly and joyously"—he looked at Willa— "eyeballing your mother."

"How did you know?" asked Nicholas.

The leaves of the apple tree fell around them. The apples were ready for picking. Summer was over.

87

"I saw her leave," said Horace, admiringly. "Her legs ended at her neck." He bit into an apple. "How *did* you know?" He leaned close to Willa, smiling.

Willa shrugged.

"I knew Wanda well," she said simply.

12

The last morning. It was cool in the attic at last, a hint of autumn to follow. The figure in the mirror looked taller. Wiser. Serene. The girl watching the figure in the mirror knew why.

You are you, Willa silently told the figure. I am me.

"What's the smile for?" asked Matthew. "Different. *You* look different somehow."

"It must be the jeans under the dress," said Willa. She pulled up the dress to show him. "No more itching."

Matthew laughed.

"Extraordinary, Willa."

The word made Willa smile. Maybe today would be

the day. The day to do something extraordinary.

"Will I see the painting today?" she asked.

Matthew shook his head. "Not today, Willa. It's my way, call it superstition. I want it completely done."

Willa nodded and watched the cats on the roof run after late-summer butterflies. Extraordinary filled her head.

"The name. What's it to be?" asked Horace at lunch.

"What name?" asked Willa.

"The baby," said Horace patiently. "The baby's name."

Willa's father drank some water.

"We have never thought about names ahead of time," he said. "We had decided that naming children was much like naming dogs or guinea pigs. You had to see them first to know."

Willa's mother nodded.

"Willa came first," she said, remembering. "Pushing and squalling into the world."

"We almost named her Fury," said Willa's father.

"You didn't!" said Willa, aghast.

"No." Her father reached over to smooth her hair. "We named you after a pioneer. The writer Willa Cather. You were, after all, *our* first pioneer into the world."

"Nicholas we named after a horse I once knew," said Willa's mother, making them laugh. She looked at them indignantly. "I loved that horse. He was pleasant and dependable, with quirks now and then."

"Such as riding too close to fences," said Willa's father, "and under low trees."

"That's true, isn't it?" Willa's mother smiled at them all. "I suspect we'll think of a name when we see the baby. Her."

"There's always Wanda," suggested Willa slyly.

"I think," said Horace, leaning his elbows on the table, "that if I were to have a child I would name her Jane."

"Jane?" Willa's mother looked at Horace.

Horace nodded.

"Jane," he said. "Straightforward and honest and calm."

"Like you," said Willa's mother, something in her tone and look causing Willa to peer at Horace more closely.

"Jane," said Horace, biting into a green Granny Smith.

Inside her house, watching the deepening shadows across the lawn, Willa waited. They had all gone off; Matthew and Horace and the Unclaimed Treasures, in a fairly obvious effort, Willa thought, to avoid the Treasures' latest experiments with cooking. This week, Horace had told Willa, it was rice. Rice cereals, rice casseroles, rice pudding desserts. "We'll all swell up and burst," he said, "and explode all over town." Willa had smiled. Horace. Straightforward and honest and calm.

Willa watched and waited. She knew they never

locked their house. And if they did, an extra key was hidden in the back shed next to the store of apples.

It was time, Willa thought. Time for her to see the painting. The face in the painting. And time to do something extraordinary. Or if not extraordinary, at least brave. She took the printed note out of her pocket.

Matthew,
I'll love you forever.
WILLA

Willa's mother was reading in the study, her father washing clothes. Fascinated, she was sure. Nicholas was upstairs working on a drawing. Slowly, quietly, Willa slipped out the kitchen door and crept across the lawn. She stood on the porch of Matthew's house and carefully pushed the front door. It swung silently in, and Willa jumped as one of the cats streaked out. Willa closed the door again and walked slowly up the stairs past the first landing, turning, and up the steep old stairs to the attic. There was a light burning in the attic room. Someone else was there.

The woman was small and slim, dressed in dark pants and a pale sweater with a touch of blue. She turned to look at Willa. Willa was not afraid. Something kept her from fear.

A moment passed.

"Are you," asked Willa wildly, filling in the silence, "another Unclaimed Treasure?"

The woman smiled, then laughed.

"I suppose I am. We are all, let us hope, unclaimed treasures." She looked closely at Willa, and Willa saw glasses perched on her head. She had been looking at the painting. "I know you are a treasure, though." She put out her hand. "You are Willa." Her gaze was steady and calm, and Willa knew suddenly. Horace's mother. *Matthew's Winnie.*

Winnie turned to look at the painting. But Willa couldn't take her eyes from Horace's mother.

"It's finished, I'm glad to see," said Winnie. "He needed to finish it." She smiled then, and there was a sinking feeling in Willa's stomach. Something final. Something startling, like when Willa had seen the picture of her mother's baby. The baby is real, she remembered thinking. *Winnie is real.*

"Well," said Winnie, lifting her shoulders in a sigh—so much like Horace—"I must go. For now."

She loves him. Winnie loves Matthew.

"Tell him," began Winnie. "Tell him . . ." But the words trailed off. She looked sadly at Willa. "Never mind, dear." And then she was gone. Leaving Willa alone in the attic room with a painting she had not yet seen.

Even before she looked, Willa was afraid. Somehow she knew. And as many times as she replayed the scene later in her mind and in her dreams, it always ended the same. The long white dress, the hat held in the hand, ribbons trailing. The face as real and alive as the face that had just stood next to her. A portrait of Winnie.

And he loves her.

Willa's eyes filled with tears and she reached up to brush them away. Not the time, she thought, for any-

93

thing extraordinary today. She saw Matthew's signature in the far right corner of the painting, small and precise. And then something else caught her eye. In the left corner were more words written. Small letters, nearly hidden in the grass beneath the apple tree.

Portrait of W

W.

A sudden movement against her leg startled Willa, and she looked down to see Blue, his tail high, his mouth open in a silent sound.

Willa sighed. W. Slowly she took the note from her pocket. Ever so carefully she tore the note, making sure that one important letter would remain. Then she propped it against the painting. Just before she turned out the light she read it.

Matthew,
I'll love you forever.
W

Willa would never remember closing the attic door, walking down the stairs and out the door. Later, the only clue, the only memory she had of what she'd done was the torn paper in her pocket with four letters printed there. ILLA.

Another stranger met. Surely the stranger most important.

13

Willa hardly slept, and the next morning her mother watched her.

"You're pale, Willa. Are you all right?"

Silently Willa nodded her head. She sipped her orange juice and finished her breakfast.

We are all, let us hope, unclaimed treasures. Winnie's words. Meaning what? Those words kept nudging Willa, pushing into her consciousness, demanding her attention. Winnie's sad face drifted into Willa's head no matter how hard she tried to forget. She thought of Matthew coming home from dinner, going up to his studio, seeing the note. She had stood at the dining-room window and watched in the darkness. The car had turned into the driveway, the inside light going on as the doors opened. Horace, Aunt Crystal, Aunt Lulu, Matthew—their faces glowing in the darkness. The kitchen light had gone on. Then the hall light. Then the attic light.

"Willa!" Her mother's voice, calling, brought her back to now. "Can you help?"

Her mother stood in the doorway.

"We need to make some casseroles. Some dinners." Her voice came from somewhere far away. "This, I think, will be the week."

Willa looked up. The week?

Her mother smiled at her, and Willa realized that her mother meant the baby. The week the baby would be born.

"Are you feeling all right?"

Her mother nodded.

"Just needing to sew up loose ends," she said.

Me too, thought Willa. If anyone could use sewn-up loose ends it is me. *We are all, let us hope, unclaimed treasures.* Willa stared at her mother as they worked in the kitchen. Her mother an unclaimed treasure? Nicholas walked into the room then. Nicholas an unclaimed treasure?

"You had better pick all the ripe tomatoes, too," her mother instructed Nicholas.

"Mother," he said, "it is not a hurricane coming. It is only a baby."

"Is that so," said his mother, smiling faintly. "The expert, eh?"

There was, for the next few days, an air of waiting.

96

Waiting for something about to happen. The baby. The show. The painting unveiled.

And there was more that would happen, too. Things unexpected that have a way of appearing and changing all that comes after. As is the way of things ordinary. Things extraordinary. Both.

There was great excitement in the hopscotch kitchen.

"There will be wine and cheese and punch and cookies and cakes at the show," said Aunt Lulu. "And music," she added.

Old Pepper sat at the table fluting seven pie crusts with a fork.

"Relax everything will be fine," he croaked.

"I, for one, cannot relax," twittered Aunt Crystal, stirring a pot on the stove. "I feel faint already. I may be falling into a decline."

"No problem if you do I can take care of that," said Old Pepper, eyeing Bella-Marie, who was perched on top of the kitchen cabinet watching for cats. "Bella fell into a decline once quite a bad one after being stuck up a chimney. She fainted dead away. I revived her nicely. Mouth-to-beak resuscitation."

Willa and Nicholas and Horace burst into laughter, though neither of the Treasures even smiled.

"That's unnatural," said Aunt Crystal, who now looked as if a decline was upon her.

"And unsanitary," added Aunt Lulu matter-of-factly, causing the three to shriek.

"What is funny?"

97

Matthew stood in the kitchen doorway. It was the first time Willa had seen him since their last morning in the attic. He reached out his hand to touch the top of Willa's head.

"What's funny?" he repeated, and to Willa's relief they began to laugh all over again as Old Pepper told his mouth-to-beak story. A bad moment passed. A step ahead, thought Willa, sighing. A page turned. For a moment, she longed for Ted and Wanda, safe in their "witless love." Willa smiled at her father's words. And then she took a breath.

"Tomorrow," she said, sounding wiser than she felt, "is the day when everything comes together."

Later, they would all remember those words.

Willa found Horace in the apple shed. It was dark and cool and damp inside, a haven from the afternoon heat. Willa could hear the sounds of the Treasures' last-minute practicing outside.

Horace sat, leaning against the dark barn boards, reading, his hand curled around an apple in the basket beside him. Willa smiled. He looked up and blinked. He smiled.

"Nicholas said you were looking for me," said Willa, sitting down beside him.

He handed her an apple.

"I have been waiting to see you alone," said Horace steadily. "I wanted to tell you a story. Two nights ago, this story starts, once upon a time. It concerns an attic room with a painting of someone whose name begins with W. And a man, the painter, who suddenly sees a note that he can hardly believe . . ."

"That's enough, Horace," said Willa, sighing. She stared at the apple in her hand, turning it over and over.

"And the man runs down the stairs," Horace went on, "and into his room and makes a phone call and talks for two hours." He turned to look at Willa. "Two hours, can you believe it?"

"Is that the end of the story?" asked Willa.

Horace nodded beside her.

"Maybe."

"How did you know?" Willa's voice was soft.

"It is like something Old Pepper once said," said Horace. " 'You may not see the horse in the barn,' he told me once. 'But you can tell he's been there.' "

Willa felt herself smile.

"My father never noticed," said Horace very softly, his breath on Willa's ear. "But *I* know the horse's printing."

Willa turned to look at him. And Horace kissed her. Straightforward and honest and calm, thought Willa, her lips smiling under Horace's, her eyes watching his. Then Horace leaned back. There was a silence in the cool apple shed.

Horace shrugged.

"Shall we kiss again?" he asked finally.

"Yes," said Willa. And they did, Willa closing her eyes at last. It was, Willa thought, lots better than a mahogany bedpost. A warm pair of human lips, she must remember to tell Nicholas. Extraordinary.

14

The day was clear, with a slight breeze. The four of them sat on the curbstone, watching the men move Matthew's paintings from the attic to the truck to the museum.

"Will there be Popsicles there?" asked Porky, who had been invited.

Horace shook his head.

"Bring some with you," he suggested. "I'm bringing apples."

Nicholas and Willa smiled for different reasons: Nicholas, because he loved the way Horace ate apples; Willa, because she loved Horace.

They got up, walking slowly up the walk, past the movers, who cursed under their breath at the awkward canvases.

"Careful!" called Matthew from the front porch, his hair mussed.

Inside the kitchen the Unclaimed Treasures were bustling and twittering. "Blathering," Horace called it, whispering in Willa's ear.

"Take the music stands," commanded Aunt Lulu. "And the music."

"And then the instruments," added Aunt Crystal, taking a last-minute cake out of the oven.

The cats, caught up in the excitement, chased each other violently, streaking across tables and whipping around corners. Blue, eyes wild, mouth agape, clung to the kitchen curtains, looking down on them all.

Bella-Marie had taken to the top of the apple tree outside, shrieking "Holiday!"

Willa found Old Pepper sitting on the back steps, taking his pulse.

"What's wrong?" she asked, alarmed.

"Making sure I'm alive that's all don't worry I do it all the time," Old Pepper reassured her.

"How do I love thee . . ." sang Bella-Marie from the treetop.

Willa saw her mother in the garden, lovingly tending her melons.

A window went up in Willa's house.

"Where are my paper clips?" yelled Willa's father.

"Probably in the left-hand drawer," Willa called back, suddenly remembering the dozens that lived in the vacuum cleaner bag. "Under your typewriter paper."

The window slammed shut again, but not before Willa heard the cries of her father as papers were caught by the breeze.

"Don't take the painting on the easel," Willa could hear Matthew calling up the stairs. "I'll take that one myself."

Willa looked up at Horace standing above her.

"Will she be there?" she asked.

Horace smiled faintly and shrugged his shoulders. "If she is, it is your doing," he said.

Willa heard the side doors of the van bang shut, the motor start. Matthew came out, balancing three pies, the flute case under his arm.

"Grab the viola, Horace." His eyes looked wild, like the cats'. "The Treasures will help hang the paintings. You all are in charge here. The last painting is still upstairs."

Aunt Lulu and Aunt Crystal came out then, handing packages and tins of cookies and pies to everyone.

"Good-bye, Wanda, good-bye, Ted," called Bella-Marie, making them all laugh.

And soon the car was packed, the doors shut on the Unclaimed Treasures.

"Peace at last," murmured Nicholas, collapsing under the apple tree.

But Nicholas was wrong. The worst of it happened

soon. Soon, amid all the peace that Nicholas had proclaimed.

"Fire!"
Willa heard it from the kitchen, where she was mixing a casserole. She ran outside, her hands still greasy.
A small wisp only. *Fire.*
Horace ran out from his kitchen, Willa's father rushing past him into Horace's house.
Horace's face was pale.
"The attic," he said hoarsely. "Smoke is coming from under the door. It's so hot," he said, staring up at Willa's mother, whose arm was around him.
Willa's father came running out the kitchen door again.
"Call the fire department," he shouted. "I'm not sure we should open the door. The fire could spread."
And then, as if they had all been struck by the thought at the same time, they looked at each other.
The painting.
Horace said it first, his face shocked at the thought.
"The tree," said Nicholas with a slight smile. *How could he smile?* But the words came to him as if they were his lines in a play. Spoken at exactly the right time.
And before anyone could stop him, he ran to the apple tree, swinging easily up into and through the impossible branches. The dangerous branches. The ones forbidden.
"Nicholas, stop!" Willa's father called to him. They

could hear, so soon, the sirens far off in the distance.

Nicholas was on the roof, moving to the windows, peering in. Suddenly he pulled his shirt over his head, wrapping it around his hand.

"Let the cats out, Horace" came a calm voice beside Willa. And it was Old Pepper, his arm around her mother. Willa saw the brown, wrinkled hand pat her mother's arm.

Horace opened the kitchen door, calling the cats. And Nicholas broke a pane of glass, reaching in to unlock the window. The fire engines came up the street and Nicholas disappeared inside while Willa held her breath. The first truck turned in the driveway, the sounds of the siren deafening. The cats were wild around her ankles. And then Nicholas was out on the roof carrying the painting, slipping slightly down the shingles to the roof edge.

"I'll have to throw it down," he called, his chest sweat marked and gleaming. And Willa saw her father run to the house as the painting, so large in the air, sailed out and over the grass to her father's feet. And then Nicholas fell, crashing noisily through the branches of the apple tree.

"Nicholas!" Willa's mother screamed.

Nicholas fell slowly, so slowly it seemed, and he landed on the ground beneath the tree.

"Watch your mother," said Old Pepper, his voice steady. He handed Willa her mother's hand as if giving away the bride. *I take thee* . . .

And then they were all looking down at Nicholas, who lifted his head a bit.

"I'm fine," he said. "Except," he added sadly, almost regretfully, apologetically, "I seem to have broken my leg." And Nicholas fainted, as gracefully as Willa had always practiced in the privacy of her room, lying back softly in the grass, closing his eyes.

15

The hospital corridor where they waited was clean and white and quiet, the silence so horrible that Willa wanted to scream. The nurses and doctors moved like white shadows up and down the hallway, in and out of doors, never looking at Willa and Horace and Old Pepper. Willa felt sick. She wondered if she threw up whether the nurses would step over it or in it or through it unnoticing. They had, she knew, not seen Bella-Marie yet, leashed to the table leg, peacefully chewing a *Newsweek* magazine. It was a year old, Old Pepper had informed them.

Horace held Willa's hand and she sat close to him, the apple in his side pocket jammed against her hip.

Willa wanted her mother and father, but they were upstairs on the maternity floor.

"Of all times," muttered Willa fiercely.

"It was the excitement that always happens," said Old Pepper, close to her on the other side, reading her thoughts. "She did not pick the time, you know."

Willa sighed and nodded, leaning her head back on the plastic chair. Her mother and father and Nicholas had all gone in the ambulance. Leaving her there. With Horace, who had held her hand as though she might run away. And Old Pepper, who insisted that he could drive.

"It's my father's car," said Willa weakly. "Are you sure?"

"Of course nothing to it," said Old Pepper. "Except for a key I think is necessary."

Willa had found the key beside the back door and, out of old habit, began a note, "Dear Mother, dear Dad," to let them know where she was going. And she had stopped, nearly bursting into tears then. They were, after all, where she was going.

"A key," said Old Pepper. "Very good a key." Then, with Willa between Old Pepper and Horace, Bella-Marie in the back, they had bumped and lurched and lunged out the driveway and over the curb into the street.

"Steering's fine," grumped Old Pepper, "but what are these little pedals down here on the floor?"

They were, explained Horace calmly, a brake and clutch. And without words he had changed places with Willa. They drove all the way to the hospital this way,

Horace working the brakes and clutch, legs all tangled, Old Pepper happily steering and making wild hand signals out the window.

"There's a directional lever there," said Horace pointing. But Old Pepper had shaken his head, preferring an arm out the window.

"Right! Turn right!" yelled Horace as Willa covered her eyes.

"Right!" shrieked Bella-Marie, flapping in the backseat.

And miraculously they turned into the hospital parking lot. Old Pepper scraped along a large black car in a space marked DOCTORS ONLY, then veered off until they came to rest against the wall of the hospital. Only a slight bump.

And now, Willa wished she were back in the car again, with the yelling, cars passing, people on the streets staring at them. It was too quiet here. And nothing was happening. *And everything was happening.*

Suddenly, Bella-Marie stood up straight, shrieking.

A nurse stopped, horrified.

"Birds of any kind are not allowed in the hospital," she said sternly.

"She is a patient," said Old Pepper just as sternly. "And I am Dr. Pepper." The nurse had stared at him for a moment, then left.

It was, finally, when Old Pepper began taking his pulse again that Willa burst into tears.

"Stop!" she cried. "Not you, too."

And Old Pepper, bony and brown and wrinkled, took Willa into his arms as Horace held fast to her hand.

And Bella-Marie, slipping her leash, wandered into the hall to pronounce each doctor to be Ted and each nurse Wanda. And the other way around.

Nicholas was pale and still. His lashes were dark against his cheeks.

"He is all right now," said the nurse, ushering them into his room, "though we had some trouble with his breathing." She eyed Bella-Marie, who eyed back.

"Nicholas," whispered Willa.

"The fire," said Nicholas, opening his eyes.

"Out," said Horace, relieved to see that Nicholas was alive. He sat on the far side of the bed and took out his last apple.

"Everything is fine everything," said Old Pepper.

"Mother?"

"Upstairs," whispered Willa, taking Nicholas's hand. "The baby's not here yet."

"Was she," began Nicholas, closing his eyes again, "in the ambulance? I didn't know. I couldn't tell."

"Yes," said Willa. "You went together."

Nicholas smiled. "I wondered. We held hands." His eyes flew open. "Not to make you jealous," he added, making Willa smile, because she had been jealous. Fiercely.

"Come back and tell me," said Nicholas.

"I will."

"I will," said Bella-Marie, sitting solemly on the foot of the bed.

"You'll see her first," he murmured just as the nurse came in.

"What? Who first?" asked Willa, leaning close.

"It's time to go, all of you, please. You too, Dr. Pepper."

As they left they could hear Nicholas begin to laugh. "Dr. Pepper," he said, laughing. "Dr. Pepper." And it was only then that Willa realized that he had meant she would see the baby first. Her sister. *Their* sister.

"And then what?" asked Willa's mother, lying back on the white sheets.

"And then Father skidded down the hall and yelled, 'It's a girl!' and we all got excited and then very bored because we knew it would be a girl. We'd forgotten."

Her mother laughed. Her hair was caught back in one of Willa's ribbons. She looked as young as Willa, which made Willa frown a lot.

"And they said we could see the baby but not you right away because you were tired," said Willa. "And everyone looked through the window at her. All except me because I didn't want to see her before Nicholas." She looked over at Nicholas, who sat in a wheelchair, his great white leg up in front of him. "They said she looked red and wrinkled like a hot prune. And then we had to go because parrots made the nurse very nervous."

"And then," said Willa's mother, turning to look at Willa, "what about the show? Matthew's."

Willa sighed.

"There were lots of people there who walked around trying to look smart and talk about paintings and colors and line and form."

"That's good," said Nicholas. "Talking of color and line and form."

"And then," Willa went on, "the Unclaimed Treasures played. But not just the two of them. There was another one. Another Unclaimed Treasure. Horace's mother, playing the violin."

"Three in a trio," said Nicholas, "after all."

Willa's mother smiled.

"And then, all of a sudden, Matthew swept down the big stairs and took the violin from Winnie's hand, and put his arms around her and kissed her with everyone looking." Willa looked at Nicholas. "For a long time he did that. Fifty-seven seconds. The Unclaimed Treasures, the other ones, kept on playing as if nothing had happened. Then Matthew bent down and whispered in Winnie's ear. And Winnie put her arms around him and rubbed his back." Willa looked at her mother, then Nicholas. "You can do that," she added. "Rub backs and kiss at the same time."

There was a silence.

"And then," said Willa, "Winnie came home. And Horace came over for dinner last night. Chicken pot pie."

They laughed.

"And that's the end of the story," said Willa softly.

"Did Matthew sell any paintings?" asked Nicholas. He sat up in the wheelchair, shifting carefully.

"Almost all," said Willa. "All but one he wished to keep."

The hospital room was filled. Filled with Unclaimed

111

Treasures, thought Willa. All except for Winnie and Matthew, home cleaning up after the fire. Probably, she mused, engaging in long and meaningful looks. Eyeballing.

The nurse finally came, lingering a bit at the door, as if delivering the secret of fire.

"She should have been an actress," whispered Horace to Willa.

"She is one," whispered Nicholas, overhearing.

"Nicholas's ears, you can tell, were not damaged in the fall," said Willa.

"So," said the nurse, placing the baby on the bed. "What do you think?"

She unwrapped the baby. And Willa nearly cried out with happiness, with joy; the baby was that ugly.

"Her hair," said Willa at last, "it is all in an uproar." *I love you, you poor thing. You poor little sister.*

"It will sit down soon," commented her father.

You are the most wonderful thing I have ever seen, thought Willa. So small, curled fingers, eyelids like rice paper.

Nicholas wheeled his chair close to the bed and reached out to touch a small hand.

"She grunts," announced Willa. *The small sounds, the whimperings of the first day.*

The baby opened her eyes, and her mouth formed an O.

Willa caught her breath.

"Willa and I love her," said Nicholas after a silence. "Though at this moment I think Willa loves her more."

Willa's mother smiled.

"I don't know if I can take all this joy," she said.

Willa's father smiled, too.

Old Pepper felt his pulse.

"Look!" cried Aunt Crystal at the window. "A great blue heron!"

"Ah," said Aunt Lulu, tripping over them all, pulling her binoculars out of her mammoth bag. "Right out the window!"

"Good-bye, Wanda, good-bye, Ted," said Bella-Marie, perched in front of the mirror, gazing at herself.

"Hello, Jane," said Willa clearly, her voice cutting through the gentle havoc of the room. Willa's mother and Horace smiled at each other. Willa put her lips on the baby's smooth dry skin. "Hello, you Unclaimed Treasure," she whispered.

"An extraordinary summer," said the man. "Apples and treasures and true loves."

"Ordinary, extraordinary," said Willa, waving her hand. "Who can tell?"

Nicholas sat in the chair opposite Willa's, stretching out his leg so that his foot touched hers.

"You still limp a little," said Willa. "Does your leg hurt often?"

"Sometimes," said Nicholas, "but as Old Pepper once said, 'I don't mind.' "

"Old Pepper," said Willa, remembering. She looked at Nicholas, her eyebrows raised.

"Yes." He nodded. "I still have Bella-Marie. She keeps me company in the studio. She has," he added, "never forgotten Ted and Wanda. She keeps a good many visitors from my door."

Willa laughed. "You cannot imagine what joy"— they both smiled at the word—"I felt when I walked by a gallery in the city and happened to look in the window and see myself upside-down there on canvas. In Papa's study. Wise Willa, you called it." Willa touched Nicholas's foot. "I stared and stared. I can still remember rain falling. A man came to stand next to me. 'That's me,' I told him. 'Me!' I read the reviews. 'An extraordinary painter!' "

"Extraordinary, ordinary," Nicholas echoed Willa's words. "I did what I did. Like you." And he held out his hand with the torn slip of paper, the words still there. ILLA. He leaned back and looked around the room.

115

"*You in this house,*" *he said, shaking his head. "Remember the first time?*"

Willa nodded. "The funeral, the undertakers, the Treasures. And the kitchen floor just fine for hopscotch. Do you know that not a day passes that I don't hopscotch through the kitchen?"

Nicholas smiled. "How long will you be here?"

"A year," said Willa, shifting in her chair. "A year, while Horace researches apples in the university orchard."

Nicholas grinned.

"A year," she went on, "while Matthew and Winnie are off in the desert, Winnie still seeking her fortune. With Matthew."

"Matthew happily painting sky and cactus and sand," said Nicholas.

"Still painting Winnie," added Willa. "Some good things don't change."

Nicholas looked up at the painting over the fireplace.

"There will be apples again soon."

Willa reached over and raised the window. The faint sound of music came to them.

Nicholas leaned forward.

"The Treasures? Playing by the garden?"

Willa nodded.

"Beethoven will always make me think of the smell of grass and apples," said Nicholas. "And of cats. The cats, Willa?"

"Gone, all of them," she said. "But there are new ones now."

Suddenly Willa sat up, brushing her hair back with her wrist.

"I think . . ." she began, her face thoughtful. "Do you have a second hand on your watch, Nicholas?"

"Time?"

Willa nodded, and Nicholas handed her his watch. He went over to the window.

"Jane," he called. Then urgently, "Get out of that tree, Jane! Find Horace!" He turned around and looked at Willa, and they began to laugh.

"The tree," said Willa, laughing. "The untrustworthy tree."

They were still laughing when Horace came, looking tall and solemn, Jane behind him. Jane's hair, Willa noticed, was sleek against her head. Willa smiled at her, caught up in an old dream. Remembering.

"What is it?" asked Horace, polishing an apple on his shirt.

"True love," murmured Nicholas, watching Willa. Which caused more laughter.

Jane, twelve and wise, looked closely at Willa. She saw the watch in Willa's hand.

"I'll call Mother," she said, and went to the kitchen. Horace stood very still.

"Do you mean the baby?"

Willa nodded and leaned back, feeling that she could stay in the big chair in the wonderful house, by the shining piano, looking at the painting, forever.

Horace came over and put his lips on Willa's forehead, where her hair began.

I should, thought Willa, and I would if I weren't

so weary all of a sudden, reach up and rub Horace's back.

"I'll drive," said Nicholas.

"A key I think is necessary," said Horace, talking into Willa's hair. And the three of them looked at each other, remembering the last time they had gone to the hospital together. And separately.

"Mother's at dance class," announced Jane in the doorway. "Papa's teaching his writing class."

She was irked, it was clear, at the laughter that came as they gathered Willa's things.

"You three laughing," she grumped. "This is important. Serious and extraordinary!" She watched her older brother, Nicholas, pick up Willa's suitcase. "Romantic, too," she told him.

"Here," said Nicholas, suddenly thrusting a piece of paper into Jane's hand. "I'll come back later and tell you a story about extraordinary things. A story with a beginning and a middle. And an end that begins another story."

The door opened.

"I-L-L-A?" Jane read slowly. "What does that mean, I-L-L-A?"

She looked up. But they were gone.

Jane sat in the chair by the window for a long time, the paper with the four printed letters in her lap, watching the moon come up over the apple tree.